# Giraffe Island

# Giraffe Island

### Sofia
Chanfreau

### Amanda
Chanfreau

Translated by Julia Marshall

GECKO PRESS

Vega
Giraffe
Island

*For Moffa,*
*founder of the first Paraphernalium.*
*For all the stories, inventions and dragon hunts,*
*and the enormous hugs that enfolded us all.*

This edition first published in 2024 by Gecko Press
An imprint of Lerner Publishing Group, Inc.
241 First Avenue North, Minneapolis, MN 55401 USA

English-language edition © Lerner Publishing Group 2024
Translation © Julia Marshall 2024
Original title: *Giraffens hjärta är ovanligt stort*
Text © Sofia Chanfreau 2022
Illustrations © Amanda Chanfreau 2022
Published originally in Swedish by Schildts & Söderströms
Published by agreement with Helsinki Literary Agency

Gecko Press aims to publish with a low environmental impact.
Our books are printed using vegetable inks on FSC-certified paper from
sustainably managed forests. We produce books of high quality with
sewn bindings and beautiful paper—made to be read over and over.

Lerner Publishing Group gratefully acknowledges the financial
support of FILI - Finnish Literature Exchange.

F I
L I

Original language: Swedish
Edited by Penelope Todd
Cover design by Megan van Staden
Typesetting by Katrina Duncan
Printed in China by Everbest Printing Co. Ltd,
an accredited ISO 14001 & FSC-certified printer

ISBN 9781776575657

For more curiously good books, visit geckopress.com

# Contents

# The giraffe has
# no vocal cords

DO YOU KNOW that giraffes have no vocal cords? That's why their necks are so long and slender compared to their bodies: there are no vocal cords swinging back and forth. If they had vocal cords, they'd have the deepest, darkest voices in the world. As long as you don't count the long-necked dinosaurs. Their voices were probably so deep the ground would shake when they spoke to each other — if they actually had vocal cords. But it hardly matters, because dinosaurs no longer exist, and it seems extraordinary to think that they once wandered around where we now build roads and houses and playgrounds.

Giraffes, on the other hand, with their dappled skin, big beating hearts and lanky necks — with no vocal cords — are as real as anything.

FAR OUT TO SEA, which could easily be the very same sea you're thinking of, there's an island shaped like a giraffe — if you look at it from above or on a map and use your imagination. It has three legs and a small tail, a large body and a long neck which ends in a head. In the middle of its body is a big lake, called Giraffe's Heart. The water in that lake is as sweet as lemonade, and the surface is almost always calm and clear, even though the salt sea around Giraffe Island storms and rages.

From the giraffe's body, the long, narrow neck runs out to the headland, and in the middle of that is the island's largest and only town, called Capital City. You might think it strange, calling a town 'Capital City' when it's not the country's capital, but since 'Capital' comes from the Latin word for 'head', it was simply too good a chance to miss. The real capital city, which is on the mainland and several times bigger than the town on Giraffe Island, had to change its name after a lot of misunderstandings, and it's now known as Kingstown.

No one lives on the rest of the giraffe's body. There are moose and blueberries that the townspeople sometimes come to shoot or pick, but it's mostly hunters, tourists and other idiots who carry on with that sort of thing. How the moose came to Giraffe Island no one knows. There are theories that they swam over from the mainland or walked across the ice. Still, you have to wonder: do moose really have such a strong sense of adventure that they'd swim straight out into the water only to see what's hidden beyond the horizon?

Because if you stand on the mainland and gaze out to sea, whether you're a moose or a person or a giraffe, you can't see Giraffe Island. And from Giraffe Island you can see nothing but sea in every direction, no matter how good your binoculars are.

If you looked at Giraffe Island from above, for example from an aeroplane or maybe from the back of an albatross, the houses in Capital City would look like small, colourful sweets scattered over the woods and red cliffs. And if you then flew lower, you'd see people, small as ants, going in and out of their candy houses, driving around in their little ant-mobiles and worrying about their various little ant problems. But of course, that's how everything looks from far away. In reality, the houses are not little sweets but real houses, and the real, normal-sized people who live in them have real, normal-sized people problems to worry about.

THERE IS A GIRL living in one of the tallest buildings in Capital City, on the top floor, which is three floors up. The girl is called Vega, and she usually sits in one of the windows, dreaming of what's across the water.

Her father had given her binoculars for her birthday. And it didn't matter to her that there was only sea to see, because in Vega's eyes the sea held almost everything. Sometimes fish and dolphins waved at her, sometimes she saw mermaids and snorting seahorses. The sea was most beautiful when the sun shone, glittering as if a wealthy lady had spilled all her pearls and jewels across its surface.

Vega would soon be ten. In her short life she'd experienced more exciting things than most nine-year-olds can ever dream of. Things that seemed ordinary to others became marvels in Vega's eyes. Her maths homework danced; the classroom turned into a castle; meals grew legs and ran double marathons, while Vega sat pecking at her food. And then there were the zebras, lions, seahorses, rhinos and all the other animals.

Many of them were hard to even find a name for, but they turned up now and then. The only trouble was, no one else seemed able to see them. Especially not Vega's father. He worried about her. You could hear it in his voice when he asked how her day had been, when he wondered why she was late home from school or why she laughed so much when she was brushing her teeth.

Vega had been laughing at the grizzly bear beside her, showering foamy shampoo from its coat, wedged into the bathtub that was far too small for it. Who wouldn't laugh?

But of course, Dad couldn't see the grizzly bear, nor any of the other animals, even though the apartment was full of them and Vega played with them all the time. Dad's eyebrows were always angled like rooftops, and dark clouds circled over his head. Sometimes the clouds began to rain, but mostly they hung over him, heavy and grey.

Vega knew that Dad's dark clouds and rooftop eyebrows were her fault, but she didn't know how to make them go away. Telling him about the animals didn't help. It seemed her father was afraid of them.

And no matter how often Vega tried to explain that the animals meant her no harm, and that she was fond of them all, her dad didn't seem to understand. It's quite hard to explain to someone who's never met a mammoth that the little woolly mammoth living in the wardrobe is actually quite friendly and lets Vega hang her clothes on its tusks. And if Vega ever woke from a nightmare, she could creep into the wardrobe and cuddle up to it. When Dad found her asleep there in the morning, his eyebrows became so steep the rain would pour off them. She tried to comfort him and get him to put his hand on the mammoth's soft fur, but he refused. He didn't think the mammoth was friendly and soft, he thought it wasn't there.

Vega had a sketchbook where she drew everything she saw. It was full of colourful animals and the funny creatures who lived in the apartment or at school or in town.

Some had names, like Atlas the asphalt beaver or Zachariah the crossing-zebra, but others were harder to name. It was easier to draw them. Vega kept her sketchbook and a pencil case full of colouring pens in her school backpack. It was good to have the book close by when she met a new animal she wanted to draw. She didn't want to leave it at home and risk Dad finding it.

When Vega was younger, she'd gone to a doctor to talk about things. Doctor Wrynk asked Vega strange questions that she answered as truthfully as she could.

Do you feel lonely? Have you any friends? It's common to have imaginary friends when you're little, and not at all abnormal. But you're not so little anymore. Do you feel abnormal?

Vega didn't really know what abnormal meant, but she definitely didn't feel alone with so many animals to keep her company. The whole time, Doctor Wrynk wrote in her notebook and nodded, her wrinkled lips stretched tight like an elastic band.

Then she asked a lot of questions about Vega's mother. Do you remember her? Do you think about her often? Do you think she thinks about you? Do you think your mother is dead?

Do you miss having a mother figure? This sounded like something Vega could make from modelling clay, which she did when she got home.

The truth was that Vega didn't know where her mother was, and she had no memory of her. She'd had only her father as long as she could remember. Sometimes she asked him what her mother was like, why she didn't live with them now and where she'd gone. But her father's answers were short and one-syllabled, and didn't sound quite true.

Besides, the clouds above her father's head began to rumble and rain whenever Vega's mother came up. So she didn't ask about her much.

EVERY MORNING, Dad took the car to his work on the other side of town. He sat there all day, looking at numbers and words, sorting paper into different-sized piles, answering the phone and using words no one could understand or care about. Vega knew this because she'd once spent a whole day at his work. Her school had decided they should have a taste of their parents' bread and butter, as they called it. All the children in the class would visit a parent's workplace for a day and then give a talk to the rest of the class. Vega didn't have much choice because she only had one parent. She bet that her mother, if she existed, would have a more enjoyable job than Dad's. Vega sat all day at her father's office playing noughts and crosses with two hyenas. Dad sat there in his suit, shushing her and the hyenas. The hyenas just laughed. If Dad had been able to see them, he would have laughed too, and thrown his tie and his papers in the air.

Dad was always home from work in time to make dinner for Vega. That was the best time of the day. They'd draw a circle in white chalk on the floor around the dining table, because Dad explained that it was best to set a boundary for anything unwelcome. Nothing strange was allowed to happen inside the line, and no creature was allowed to join

them. It worked well; all the animals waited outside the circle and let Vega and her father eat in peace. As he served up the meal, he always asked how her day had gone. Vega knew exactly how to answer.

'The usual. Pretty normal.'

'Nothing out of the ordinary then?'

'No, just ordinary.'

'And how did the maths test go?'

'Absolutely fine. I let the octopus do it—he writes so fast with all those arms.'

Dad's eyebrows became steep roofs.

'I mean, he sat beside me. Of course, I wrote it myself. I got them all right, I think.'

The rooftops became less steep.

'Good. Well then.'

The forks went scrape, scratch on their plates. Dad smiled at Vega and his clouds almost evaporated.

It'd been like this for as long as Vega could remember. Monday spaghetti, Tuesday beetroot soup, Wednesday fish, Thursday cauliflower cheese, Friday curried stew. Next week the same thing. Bedtime songs and lights out at the same time every night. Dad operated like clockwork. Vega knew exactly what to expect. And that was more than could be said about the rest of her life.

But in the last few weeks, something had changed. Summer had turned into autumn, school had started and something had also happened with Dad.

WHIM, WHAM, it was as if the wind had changed, and flipped everything upside down. Dad had come home late from work many evenings in a row. First, he was late with dinner. The beetroot soup was cold and the spaghetti undercooked. He didn't notice. The clouds circled above his head in unfamiliar patterns, white and blue and grey. He ate quickly, muttered, looked down at his plate, stared out the window. He was listening to something outside the chalk circle, but not to Vega. He didn't even ask about her day as he usually did. Vega told him anyway.

'It was quite an ordinary day today, Dad.'

'Mm.'

'A zebra helped me with dictation. It went really well.'

'Mm. That's good.'

No change in the clouds.

'It was actually the zebra who wrote the whole dictation for me,' Vega continued. 'The zebra's very good at spelling, except that it changed all the Ss to Zs. But the words looked much more fun with Zs, so it didn't matter. Zun zhinez in the zummer.'

'Mm. Nice.'

'At break I skipped with two rubber monkeys. It was fun until one of them tripped on the rope and grazed its knee. I had to stay and help him bandage it, so I missed geography.'

'Mm. Good.'

The animals peered in, big question marks stuck in their

fur. What was going on? When even a yellow-and-green striped hippo thinks something is strange, you know things are not right.

Dad started coming home even later, long past dinner time. He made excuses and pulled out frozen dinners that he'd thaw in the oven. They tasted like nothing mixed with sawdust.

The goodnight song was mumbled or abandoned completely. But it didn't matter how the food tasted or that dinner was late (Vega had already been served sandwiches by a giggling ostrich, and she could sing the goodnight song to herself) — it was Dad's behaviour that was so worrying.

He was somehow far away, which is a strange way of describing someone sitting opposite you at the dining table, but that was the best Vega could come up with. Several football fields further away with each passing day.

# An octopus has
# three hearts

IF YOU TAKE the path past the reservoir, up the hill, past Lotsstugan where the famous banjo player Ylva String grew up, and then follow the cliff edge with the forest on one side and a gaping drop to the water on the other, you'll come eventually to a yellow fence. You can also take the gravel road on the other side of the mountain to get there, which is quicker and easier. But Vega preferred to take the path past Lotsstugan when she went to see Hector. The animals she met up on the mountain were exciting and different, often camouflaged as rocks or trees. A rocky outcrop would suddenly quiver and give rise to a herd of mossy stone lions, or green hedgehogs as big as Saint Bernards would scuttle about under the spruce trees.

Hector was Vega's grandfather. Fantastic things always happened when she visited him. Vega went to his house after school. With Hector she could be exactly as she wanted. She didn't need to pretend or make things up; Hector believed everything she said. He'd laugh so hard the gold teeth at the back of his mouth gleamed, and he fished his big ears out from under his hair to listen to what she had to say.

He asked about the animals she'd met that day, how they were doing, and suggested she invite them for coffee next time they turned up.

Hector never worried about Vega. He had no clouds over his head and his eyebrows were never steep like rooftops. His nose was as big as an eagle's beak, with a little swing-up at the bottom, like a ski jump. Hector was old, but he had almost no wrinkles, except sun wrinkles round his eyes when he laughed – which was most of the time. Hair was heaped on his head like a golden helmet, and although it looked silky-soft, Vega knew it was so thick you could hardly run your hand through it.

Hector's arms were spotty in the way many old people's arms can be. But there was one spot that was special. At first glance, it looked like any old mark. But if you looked more closely, and upside down, it was a little fuzzy giraffe with no ears. What was extra special about the birthmark was that Vega had one almost the same on her own arm. 'That's how we know I'm your grandfather,' Hector would say. 'Only funny people like us have such fine markings.'

Coming through the gate in the yellow fence was like stepping into another world: from the mountain's barren pines and straggly blueberry bushes into the most luxuriant garden you can imagine.

Hector's garden was unlikely but also likely if you knew him. There were blackberry bowers and mango hedges, lilacs and apple blossom, buddleias and fir trees, banana groves and rhododendrons, liquorice ferns and ruby leaves, plankton maples and dadya trees, and everything bloomed and bore fruit at the same time.

Animals lived there too. Very strange animals. There were rabbits with no ears, stripy mice, horses as small as cats and beetles as big as guinea pigs. Not to speak of all the animals impossible to describe, like frudbimbles and spoonlurks, fasterers and fourfentipedes. And others with no names, which Vega drew in her sketchbook.

Hector watered the whole garden with lemonade and set out small bowls of juice for the animals.

Hector's house was in the middle of the garden. From outside, it looked like a box. But when it rained, all the surfaces swelled with water, the roof stretched to form a dome, and the topmost white corners of the house grew into towers and pinnacles. Inside, the walls shot up and the corners rounded out, spiral staircases grew from nowhere to reach new storeys, with a crisp sound like the cracking of spring ice; all the surfaces were instantly coated in gold and the house became a palace.

'It's this confounded humidity,' Hector complained as he served Vega tea and apple pie on the newly emerged crystal veranda.

When the sun shone, the house took on a completely different form. The walls dried and shrank, and large cracks formed between the planks. The roof collapsed into firewood. In the end, the house looked like a little hut.

'It's this confounded drought,' Hector complained, and he and Vega stayed out in the garden.

Hector always went about with a wheeled trolley. It had a seat in front, a bit like a kick sled, and a shelf on top. He said it was practical: he could keep small things he liked close to hand. For example, a roll of tape, an extra light bulb, bandages, throat lozenges, warm socks and a hat.

'Life's too short to run around looking for your hat the whole time,' said Hector, 'which is why you need a nifty trolley like this to keep it in.'

Hector often had visitors. Several times a day a car would drive up the long road on the other side of the mountain, and a couple of keen-eyed figures in white coats would hop out.

'Ah, here are my agents again! Time for the afternoon report,' said Hector, wheeling his trolley to the front door.

'Good day, sir,' said the white-coated agents. Vega thought it was very smart of the agents to wear white coats. You'd never guess they were agents if you didn't know.

'Here we are again. How are things with Hector?'

'Thanks,' answered Hector, 'absolutely excellent, as they were last time! And I understand you're working very hard; I hope you've got a little further in your investigation.'

One of the white coats laughed. 'You could say that. Has Hector remembered his medicine today?'

'Ah, my visibility pills! Of course, I took them a moment ago. Before that I wasn't exactly invisible, but a little blurry round the edges. Come with me so we can prepare your report. Vega, wait here, we'll be back soon!'

Hector had so much going on. Even though he was old, he could manage various top-secret investigations, look after his fantastic garden with all the animals and know everything there was to know in the whole world. He knew all the stories and legends about Giraffe Island, and they grew more exciting every time he told them. Sometimes they were about the faceless men who once lived on the outskirts of Capital City, who painted eyes, a nose and a mouth on their faces every time they went out. Sometimes they were about the knight with a green beard who planted the whole forest on the island using the hairs of his beard for seedlings. Or the humplefoot, the enormous creature almost impossible to see, who according to Hector wandered around this very forest. He'd seen where its footprints created great pools in the bog. Sometimes Hector told her about Giraffe's Heart, the most beautiful lake in the whole world. The water in the lake was as sweet as lemonade, but not many people knew that. Giraffe's

Heart was so shallow you could wade across without the water going above your knees, and also so deep that no one had ever found the bottom, Hector said. Sometimes a sea creature and an underwater city appeared in the story. Other times there was nothing living or growing at Giraffe's Heart; it was like a gigantic bathtub. No one knew for sure, Hector said.

Vega could ask Hector anything. It wasn't always clear what he meant, but he always had an answer, and more.

'Hector?'

'Yes, small figment of my imagination?'

'Why is Giraffe Island called that?'

'Because it looks like a giraffe! Especially if you see it on a map.'

'But why is it drawn like a giraffe on the map?'

'Because people who draw maps have special methods to determine what land looks like from above. They send out a large flock of albatrosses, and they can tell the shape of the land by the types of cries the birds make.'

'So, albatrosses call out that the island looks like a giraffe?'

'Exactly. I was involved in an albatross survey once. It was top-level technology. Of course, it works even better with eagles, but we don't have those here.'

'What does the mainland look like?'

'Probably like any old mainland. I think it has the shape of a crooked old woman, if I remember rightly. But they only have small birds to help with their map work, so who knows what it actually looks like.'

'Have you ever been there?'

'Yes, probably, I dare say I have.'

'Don't you remember?'

'Yes, of course I do.'

'Do you remember my mother then?

'Oh yes, very well. Hm, let me see, she looked a bit like this.' Hector pointed to a small, faded picture that hung over the fireplace. It was a photo of a young girl who looked a little like Vega, with dark curly hair and dark eyes looking anxiously at the camera. She was wearing an oversized green coat; the arms covered her hands and the hem trailed on the ground. On her head was a large top hat. Hector always pointed to the photograph when Vega asked about her mother.

'But Hector, my mother can't look like that now. That's just a little girl.'

'Yes, a little girl, that's right,' Hector mumbled. 'She loved dressing up in my clothes.'

Hector's eyes glistened and looked past the photograph, past the fireplace, out through the walls and into a world not even Vega could see.

'But what was she like?'

'Your mother? Lovely, a very lovely person. But she had a fiery temper, she could flare up like a woodstove when she was small.'

'But what's she like now? And where is she?'

'Good question. Hard to say. Pretty sure the coat fits her better now.'

That was about as far as Vega got when she asked about her mother. Hector who knew everything seemed to have forgotten almost everything about her mother.

Vega's mother was like a paper doll in Vega's imagination, one she could dress in new clothes and accessories for each new thing she learned about her. But she didn't know many things, and it was a long time since she'd given the doll a new accessory.

It had been wearing a green coat and top hat for a long time. It also had curly hair, and wings, so it could fly away when it wanted to. Sometimes the wings became flames. Hector had said that her mother was fiery. Maybe the paper doll should be a dragon, one that could breathe fire and fly. A paper kite dragon that could fly up, up. Without a string.

THEY SAT IN THE GARDEN drinking Hector's home-made honey and skyberry juice. It was warm and sunny, so Hector's house had shrunk once again to a little hut. There wasn't much to be done about it, other than to stay in the garden and hope for a few drops of rain. Vega had gone straight to Hector after school. She knew that her father wouldn't be home anyway. As usual.

'Hector?'

'Yes, small figment of my imagination,' replied Hector, blowing large pink bubbles of skyberry juice through a straw. They sailed far away through the garden, until a flock of joybells fluttered out of a bush and attacked them.

'Dad's been behaving strangely,' said Vega.

'He's always behaved strangely.' Hector patted a passing firefly. 'At least, I've never understood what makes that man tick.'

'No, but it feels as if something has happened. I don't know what. He's almost never home, and even when he is, he's not really there. He hardly listens to anything I say, and he forgets to cook dinner.'

'Aha! I understand exactly,' said Hector. 'He must have had a heart attack! They say it can happen. It makes you all confused and dizzy and you forget things.'

'But he's not sick, just strange.'

'Well, that's exactly what happens with a heart attack. Try to listen to his heartbeat next time you see him. I bet it sounds different than it used to. It might be broken. Kaput!'

Vega thought about her father's heart, broken into a thousand pieces. If it had broken, it would surely mean more bad luck than breaking a mirror.

'But how would it break?' she asked.

'It can break in many different ways. It's tricksy, the heart. Be glad you're not an octopus; they have three!'

'Is that true?'

'Of course it's true! It's quite practical, because if you have three hearts, they can take turns being broken and healed. Octopuses must be very happy animals.'

Vega imagined a very happy octopus with three different hearts blinking red, yellow and green, like traffic lights.

Red meant broken, green meant healed, and yellow something in between.

'Your father may not have three hearts,' said Hector, 'as far as we know. But at least he has one, and it's big. So he has to take extra care. A bit like having a huge china shop. In a normal-sized china shop you can keep an eye on everything all the time, but if it's huge, it's much harder! Maybe a whole elephant is hiding in the basement. And it's trampled to pieces your most valuable porcelain bowls, but you don't know it. You might only find out much later and realise they've been broken for ages. Well, you get the logic. It's exactly the same with your father.'

Sometimes Hector's logic was too convoluted for Vega. She nodded silently and swallowed a gulp of skyberry juice.

# Rhinos have
# pink milk

NORMALLY THE WALK to school was a meandering adventure with all sorts of exciting animals to greet, but today the road was straight, and the animals didn't take much notice of Vega. An asphalt beaver lay asleep at a crossing. Vega bent down and scratched it under its chin. It was usually asleep when Vega passed on her way to school because asphalt beavers are known to be late risers. During winter, they sleep almost the whole time, but on a sunny autumn day like this one, they would normally get up and gnaw on the curb, at least, before lunch.

Her father had been home when Vega returned from Hector's the evening before. His shoes and jacket were tossed on the hall floor and a packet of spinach patties lay on the kitchen table.

'Oven's on!' Dad called from his office.

The oven wasn't on. Vega took off her coat and crept up to Dad's office. She opened the door a crack. There he sat with his papers like a wild ocean around him.

'Won't we eat dinner together?' Vega asked.

'I haven't got time, Vega,' said Dad as he dived deeper into the sea of paper. 'I'm behind with work. What say you have a few spinach patties, then go and do some skipping in the garden? You're so good at it.'

Dad's phone rang. He hunted for it among the four thousand pieces of paper and motioned with his coffee cup for Vega to close the door.

Vega sighed, remembering this as she gave the crossing-zebra a handful of gravel. It stretched and let Vega skip across the street on its stripes.

So maybe there really was something wrong with her father's heart. It seemed more likely now Vega thought about it. After her visit with Hector, she couldn't stop picturing the big elephant rampaging in his heart, smashing the forgotten porcelain bowls. Who was the elephant? Where had it come from? Vega wondered if she should ring the hospital and ask if it was usual for someone to behave like Dad after a heart attack. But maybe she should ask him first. Today after school she'd wait for him at home, and really try to listen to his heart as Hector had suggested. It shouldn't be too hard, if she could just hug him long enough before he wriggled away.

SCHOOL WAS A yellow stone building from the olden days, built in the complicated and impractical way that old buildings often are. It was in the middle of Capital City, on top of a hill. The building clung to the summit like a tight-fitting, oddly shaped yellow hat. There were many windows, tall and narrow, with coloured glass illustrating famous tales or funny local stories. The gutters running from the slate roof to the ground were shaped like animals: lions, pigs, horses and snakes, their bodies stretching into pipes along the wall. At the bottom, their mouths opened wide; stiff, tired mouths forever spouting water over the hillside.

The corridors inside the building went in zigzags rather than straight lines, just to create more corners for pedestals you could place busts on. The ceiling in the broom closet was painted with angels and seraphim, and the floor was covered with beautiful mosaics, even in the toilets.

You could call the school Grandiose. At least that's its middle name. Its full name is Giraffe Island's Grandiose Primary School, but most of the time it's simply called 'school'.

The third years' classroom was off a long corridor on the first floor. The classrooms were called Schooner, Brig and Galleon, and were decorated with all kinds of marine objects. Schooner was rigged out like a ship, with lifebuoys, fishing nets and ropes along the walls. In Galleon there was a figurehead right beside the blackboard, and Brig was

equipped with a huge ship's wheel so you could pretend you were out at sea, steering a great ship.

It was time for Fun Hour in Schooner. Fun Hour was one hour a week when anything could happen. It could be charades, a film; sometimes the children were allowed to pretend they were at sea in a raging storm. Vega loved Fun Hour. And today, something extra fun was going to happen.

'Fun Hour starts. . . NOW!' cried Ms Hum, and the whole class fell silent. Ms Hum was a large woman, who wore her hair pulled into a tight knot on top of her head and garish dresses that reminded Vega of Hector's garden. She was strict and not especially nice, but Vega liked her. Ms Hum's piercing gaze could put any troublemaker in their place, and her voice was hard as a whip. But if you met her gaze you could see – through about eight layers of rigidity – a small friendly light. Vega knew that Ms Hum was essentially kind. She was like an onion with many layers to peel off (that sometimes made you cry). And she looked like a rhino.

'Today at Fun Hour you'll be assigned a pen pal,' Ms Hum announced, with a sigh of boredom. 'You will go on to exchange letters with said pen pal for the whole term. One letter a week, which I will read, correct and post. No cheating!'

A pen pal. A friend. This Fun Hour had started well.

'So, you may each pick a letter from my basket. The children who have written to you almost all come from the mainland. Well, all but one who is trying to be different and doesn't go to school at all.'

Ms Hum sighed and mumbled something about loose rules, home schooling and hot potatoes.

'These mainlanders have written letters to you all without knowing who the recipient will be. It is up to you to reel in the friendship offered with this juicy bait. How will you achieve that? How do you write a good letter? Well, I'm going to tell you.'

Vega gripped her pencil. She'd been waiting for the day they'd learn how to make friends.

Ms Hum wrote on the board – her handwriting unexpectedly curly for someone so stern – muttering every second word out loud. When she'd finished, she threw the pen on the floor. The board read:

How to write a successful letter
1. Begin with an opening phrase. *Hello, Good day or Dear* . . . are acceptable.
2. Show interest in the other person. Ask how they are doing or how they feel. Feel free to give a compliment.
3. Comment on everything your pen pal told you in their previous letter. If they wrote that they were going on a trip, ask how it went.
4. Tell them about yourself. Your hobbies, your family, the books you've read. Be sure to ask another question for each thing you tell – your pen pal may get bored if you write only about yourself.

5. Draw a picture if you are good at drawing, otherwise, don't.
6. Finish with a sign-off phrase, such as *Yours sincerely* or *Best wishes* — or for the more ambitious, why not *Auf Wiedersehen* or *Au revoir?*

Vega wrote everything in her notebook as fast as she could.

Then Ms Hum went around the classroom with her basket. It was full to the brim with envelopes with no addresses on the outside, only things like 'from Karl' or 'To an islander' or nothing at all.

When Ms Hum came to Vega's desk, Vega's hand hovered mid-air. So many future friends, but she could only choose one. Isaac, who sat beside her, reached across and grabbed a letter at random.

'Hurry up now, Vega,' said Ms Hum. 'It's called Fun Hour, not Fun Year.'

A letter in the depths of the basket looked out at Vega. It was a little wrinkled and dirty and had nothing written on the outside. It was beating like a heart. Vega reached for it, past all the other letters waiting and yawning. The letter beat even harder and flew into her hand.

A letter just for her. She couldn't remember ever receiving a letter in her life, except for the ones Hector sometimes hid in his mail bottle tree, which Vega was allowed to open and read when the bottles around them were ripe. It was always exciting, even though she knew Hector had written them all. But now she'd received a real letter, one that came in the post, from her very own friend. She hurried to open it.

Hello Someone!
How are you? I'm fine. Who are you?

My name is Janna, and I am nine years and two months old. I live in a circus. We travel around the world putting on shows. I don't perform myself — I can only juggle a little bit. But my mothers work here, so I have to travel with them. I have two, as if one wasn't enough. One is called Katja and she's the circus director. She also makes sure I do my homework, she's like my teacher. My other mother is called Phoenix and she works with the circus animals.

Is it fun living on an island? Do you have an ordinary life? Do you have many ordinary friends? I'd like to go to a normal school with classmates and playtime. It's not as much fun as you might think living with a circus. There are hardly any children and you can never make new friends because we travel to a new place every week.

Do you have any pets? I don't, although there are lots of fun circus animals I can play with, but only when Phoenix is there. I'd love to have a dog or maybe budgies.

I'm glad we'll be friends, even though I don't know who you are. I'm writing the address we'll be at next week, so you know where to send your letter.

Regards,
Janna

Vega read the letter three times. It was the best thing she'd ever read. To think, here was someone just like her. How was it possible that someone who lived in a circus, which must be the best place in the world to live, could long for something as boring as going to a normal school? And how could life be so unfair that Janna had two mothers when Vega had none at all?

Ms Hum wandered the classroom again with her basket, this time filled with pieces of coloured paper and glue and crayons and calligraphy pens for anyone who wanted to make a good impression on their new pen pal. The more beautiful the letter, the better your friendship will be, said Ms Hum.

Vega chose gold tissue paper she could fold up into flowers. And a lot of glitter glue for sticking them to the paper. Janna's letter lay beating on the desk. Vega chose the finest calligraphy pen, and wrote in her best handwriting:

Hello Janna!
How are you? I am fine. I like your name!

My name is Vega. I live with my father in a three-storey apartment building in Capital City, Giraffe Island. Have you ever been in an apartment building? My father is nice most of the time. I don't have a mother at all, or at least I don't remember her. How lucky to have two of them. And to live in a circus!

It's not so much fun going to a normal school. I'd rather live in a circus. But it's okay here.

In my spare time I like visiting my grandfather and running around his garden and drawing. What do you like doing? Do you like drawing?

I have a lot of pets, but none that my father knows about. I'd like a dog. I think Dad would too, although he says he's busy enough already with me. My father is never really happy. I think he'd be better with a pet he could see. Or maybe a mother.

Here is a drawing I've made of the spotted rhinoceros that was sitting eating ice cream the other day in the school dining room. Did you know that rhino milk is

pink? My grandfather told me. I don't know if it's true, but
they seem to like ice cream at least.

I hope to hear from you soon!

Yours sincerely,

Vega

When Vega had finished her letter, she went to Ms Hum's
desk, where she sat with her red pen ready. She read Vega's
letter with her eyebrows raised and then wrote a number
in her book.

'Simple but worth reading,' she said.

Butterflies fluttered madly in Vega's stomach as she
walked back to her seat.

VEGA WAS SO excited by what had happened in Fun Hour,
she almost forgot the important mission waiting for her at
home. The butterflies in her stomach fluttered, about Janna
and circuses and exciting times ahead. It felt as if they might
lift her whole body off the ground and fly her away. The sun
cast long rays over the street and sun-cats danced along the
lawns, their tails keeping time. The asphalt beavers were
digging gravel ponds in the pavement, so she had to zigzag
between them. Vega laughed. She couldn't wait to tell her
father about Janna.

At a traffic light an octopus clung with its many arms,
blinking its three hearts at her. Green, yellow, red. Then
she remembered. Dad's heart.

Vega was almost at the steps to the apartment when her feet stopped abruptly. A strange car was parked outside. It was white and shiny with crooked eyes that were looking at nothing. Something gleamed in the sun by the front tyre. Vega went close and bent over. It was... ice. The air was warm, with the lingering breath of summer. Birds were chittering in the trees. But on the ground by the white car's tyre, there was a small, mirrorlike patch of ice.

Vega closed the door very carefully behind her as she entered the apartment. Her father was home. Low voices came from the kitchen. No frying pan, no sizzling, no smell of dinner. A chilly gust along the hall made Vega shiver.

'Vega, is that you?' Dad's voice.

Vega made herself like wallpaper, but she took a few steps closer to the kitchen.

'Are you there? Come in, Vega, there's someone I'd like you to meet.'

Vega took the last steps to the kitchen door. Her father sat at the table, the rain clouds in disarray and a plate of crumbs in front of him. Beside him sat a woman with long black hair and bright eyes. She looked at Vega and smiled. Another cold gust went through Vega's body.

'Vega,' said Dad, 'this is Viola.'

# Frogs drink through their skin

ON THE EDGE OF TOWN — not the same edge as Hector's house — was an abandoned area with old factory buildings. The factories were no longer in use because almost everything sold on Giraffe Island now came from the mainland on large barges packed with boxes. The buildings were surrounded by dusty grass that was never mowed, crooked trees and piles of scrap. Many of the buildings' windows were broken and you could glimpse old, rusted machines inside that no one knew how to use anymore. Rats and voles had built nests inside the furnaces and control rooms, and escaped hamsters used gears and old conveyor belts as exercise equipment.

Only one factory appeared to be still in business, at least perfect smoke rings rose every night from a corner of the building. It was the old toothpaste factory.

It lay between the old cake factory and a large meadow, and, like the other factory buildings, it was overgrown with trees and ivy that twined between the bricks. But if you were out strolling in the evenings in the abandoned factory area — not many were besides the local rats and deer — you'd see light shining from the topmost windows. And even if passersby didn't notice the smoke rings or the lights, they couldn't fail to hear the music pouring from the top floor of the toothpaste factory every night.

This was where Nelson Frank lived. The music came from the kitchen radio, which his mother turned on when she got home from work. She always looked for the station with the most music because she hated hearing people talk, she said. Then she'd turn the radio to maximum volume, open the kitchen window and light a cigarette. Mrs Frank was clever at blowing smoke rings; they sailed out the window into the air like fluffy dream donuts. She could blow as many as she wanted in a row. If she was in the right mood, she could blow squares, which Nelson sometimes tried to catch in glass jars. His mother had a dry laugh that she used sometimes to blow out smoke in the form of a smile. This was rare, though, so Nelson had only one jar with smoke-smiles. He'd collected quite a few jars with smoke squares and a whole cupboardful of jars with various sizes of smoke rings.

Nelson had a whole room of jars and boxes and drawers, filled with different collections. There was a shelf where

he'd collected grains of sand with a particular shape, a box of old burst balloons, and a whole folder of used scratch tickets he'd found on the ground. He also had several matchboxes of dead spiders resting on beds of cotton wool, and an extremely impressive collection of dust bunnies in an old shoebox. He was very proud of this collection and handled it with the greatest care so the dust bunnies wouldn't fall to pieces.

Nelson also took an old tape recorder with him everywhere. He used it to record funny laughs. He had thirty-two. Number sixteen was his favourite. It belonged to Ms Hum, who once began to laugh hysterically when a boy in the class fell over his own shoelace and fell splat on the floor in the middle of Fun Hour. Ms Hum's laugh sounded like a gravel-scooping digger, and it made Nelson laugh every time he played it. Another favourite was number three, which belonged to his father. Mr Frank had a big, boisterous laugh, like drumbeats on an empty barrel.

But most important in Nelson's collection was his notebook, which he always kept in his pocket. The notebook was red and worn, held together with a shoelace. The cover was engraved in deeply pencilled letters which said: *Nelson's Interesting Facts*. Nelson had written this in the most decorative letters he could think of. He'd had the book for years, and in it he wrote down every interesting, unusual thing he'd come across. There were many facts about animals because Nelson spent more time with animals than with people. And animals do many peculiar things. People do too, but they can be harder to observe because people are often cleverer than animals at hiding their eccentricities. Nelson had a whole page in his book about frogs. He'd written, for example, that Frogs cannot swallow with their eyes open and Frogs drink by absorbing water through their skin. Nelson had learned these things by lying on his stomach for a whole day on the edge of a pond in the forest with his magnifying glass.

*Nelson's Interesting Facts* included facts about spiders, badgers, moths, maths teachers, gravel, blowfish, paper, budgies, mothers, dirt, hamsters, space, ice creams on sticks, dogs, telephones, wire, snakes, love, sparrows, cars, snails, hairs, giraffes and acorns. If everyone had Nelson's book, no one would need to go to school.

Nelson had no brothers or sisters, but he had a dog. And not just any old dog. A cross between Unknown and Enormous, she was called Flor. She had short, golden-brown fur that curled at her throat, friendly eyes and soft ears. And she was as big as a small horse. Nelson had ridden her to school until a couple of years ago, but this last year his legs had grown so long that his feet dragged on the ground when he sat on Flor's back. Nelson was the tallest in their year group. On the other hand, he'd repeated the year a couple of times.

It was the giant dog Flor who made sure that Nelson got to school on time. She woke him, helped him dress (always in the same pale blue overalls) and put out cornflakes and milk. Flor put the boy's clothes in the wash and clipped his nails when they got too long. Flor had always been the one to do all this. It wasn't that Nelson's mother didn't care. She did, in her way. It was just that Flor cared more.

So Nelson was in Vega's year but not in the same class. Nelson was in Brig, the classroom beside Schooner. Schooner and Brig had the same teacher, Ms Hum, who went back and forth between classes, setting tasks. Sometimes she couldn't manage the back and forth, so she shouted extra loud through the wall. Often she shouted Nelson's name, because she knew Nelson was probably up to something on the other side of the wall—even if she couldn't see it. It was always Nelson.

It wasn't his fault that there were so many more fun things to do than go to school. None of the books they read in class were as interesting as *Nelson's Interesting Facts*. And none of the other kids in the class seemed to know any of Nelson's interesting facts — which was shocking, honestly — so Nelson was constantly having to tell them all kinds of things. It wasn't his fault, was it, that he still hadn't learned to tell the time, and was always late to class? Or, for the same reason, that he didn't get to bed, but stayed up all night; surely that wasn't the worst that could happen? There were so many exciting things to do at night. If only Ms Hum knew. Nelson would run and hunt fireflies with a net in the trees around the factory buildings or count

snores from his parents' bedroom. After a hundred he got
to eat a raisin. If his father was home there were a lot more
raisins in the night, but if he wasn't then Nelson had to
make do with one every ten minutes or so.

NELSON WAS ALWAYS on the lookout for more fun facts
to write in his book. Sometimes he just wandered around
town looking at things. He never kept track of where he
was, and even though it was a small town and he'd lived
there all his life, he never learned to find his way. Maybe
it was because he was usually looking down at the ground
or up at trees instead of straight ahead. Flor kept an eye on
where they ended up and led him home to the toothpaste
factory when he got hungry or tired.

Every afternoon, Flor waited for him at the edge of the
forest outside school. She lay hidden a little way in among
the trees, so the other children wouldn't find her during
breaks. People, especially adults, were often afraid when
they saw her because she was so big. Once Ms Hum had
been standing at the bottom of the school steps just as Flor
dropped Nelson off on the edge of the forest. Nelson had
slid from Flor's back and given her a hug. Ms Hum gasped
and dropped her basket, scattering apples and folders in
the gravel. She was about to scream. Flor hid as fast as she
could in the undergrowth. Ms Hum trembled and clenched
her fists. And although she might have wanted to shriek,

'Help! A giant dog! Police!' what came ringing out was: 'Nelsoooon!!'

Flor settled down in a thicket. She didn't mind that others were afraid of her. All she wanted was to be with Nelson, and make sure he was all right.

Flor, unlike Nelson, had an excellent sense of direction, and could find her way home to the toothpaste factory from anywhere in town. Recently, Nelson had started circling Lotsberget, close to the ferry dock. There were apparently many interesting animals for him to investigate. He went there every day after school and didn't go home till dark. No matter how high up the mountain he roamed, zig-zagging between pine trees and thickets with his nose to the ground, the dog always had her eye on him.

# 5

# Starfish have no brains

VEGA HAD FOUND the elephant. The one that was rampaging around, breaking all the fragile things in her father's heart. Viola. Where had she come from? What did she want?

It was a week since Vega came home from school and saw the white car and the patch of ice for the first time. Now the car was parked there almost every day, white and shiny with its shifty eyes. And the patch of ice had grown. The whole apartment was colder since Viola had turned up. Icy winds blew along the hall even when all the windows were closed, and opening the fridge felt like opening the door to a tropical summer. Vega would stand at the open fridge door and warm herself when Viola was around. Dad didn't seem to mind the cold. The clouds above his head were mostly white like cotton balls, but with a streak of frost. They were almost completely still, but sometimes light flakes of snow drifted from them. His eyes looked far away.

Vega had tried listening to her father's heart, as Hector had suggested. She'd crept up behind him one evening while he sat muttering over a book and put her ear as close as she could without touching him. A dull thump like a tennis ball against a wall. There didn't seem to be anything wrong with the way his heart was beating; it ticked along at a regular pace. But he wasn't himself anymore. He'd changed.

The chalk circle he used to draw on the kitchen floor when they ate dinner was smudged and forgotten. Without that clear boundary, the animals roamed freely around the table, pinching food from plates whenever they felt like it. But her father didn't notice. He'd stopped singing for her at night. Vega knew she was really too big for lullabies. But the goodnight song was one of the things she'd shared with him. They ate dinner together, and they had their song. He'd come into her bedroom at the same time every night when she was already under her duvet, to turn out the light. It was a simple song, which he sang slowly and a little off-key, but it was the most beautiful song Vega knew.

> *When the sun's gone down,*
> *all I can't see takes a life of its own.*
> *Morning always turns to night,*
> *whatever begins comes to an end,*
> *up goes down and in comes out.*

*I know what it means:*
*soon the day I'm waiting for will come.*

But now he hadn't sung it for several weeks. He'd gone off somewhere above the clouds. And Vega had no idea how to pull him down again.

Viola's presence in the apartment really was like an elephant in a china shop. Everything beautiful had been broken, and it was impossible to carry on as usual. And Vega couldn't talk to her father about it, because Viola was there almost all the time. Some of Vega's animals had also retreated, barely venturing out of her room. They huddled in there, holding each other, growing thick fur to keep out the cold. Some days only the polar bears showed up. But they didn't want to go into the hall either, let alone the kitchen, and if they caught sight of Viola they rushed back into Vega's room and closed the door. As if Viola could see them.

Viola might have been beautiful, at least if Vega had seen her in a painting. Her skin was pale, almost translucent in places, like on her neck where you could see thin veins branching down to the pit of her throat. But her veins weren't lilac or blue like normal veins, instead they gleamed like silver through her skin. She had a sharp outline, as if she'd been drawn in black felt pen, and her jet-black hair flowed down her back like a soft veil. Her eyes were as bright as stars. You couldn't look into them because they shone so fiercely. Vega couldn't see anything for several minutes when she'd tried.

But Viola wouldn't leave her alone. She persisted in asking Vega all sorts of questions, wondering how things were at school and whether she liked pancakes, what books she liked and what was her favourite film. Vega wished Viola wouldn't try to be nice. She wanted her to disappear, so everything could go back to normal.

Vega hadn't told her father about her new pen pal, Janna. Before, she'd have talked about nothing else. Vega would have shown Janna's letter to Dad as soon as she came home from school and he would have brightened up, with maybe even a little sun appearing in the clouds above his head. But Viola's presence had built an ice wall between Vega and Dad. She couldn't talk to him anymore, not even to tell him she'd found a friend. She'd almost forgotten it herself.

That's why Vega didn't know at first what kind of envelope it was that lay quivering in the hall when she came home one day. It didn't look like the envelopes beside it, which had windows with her father's name in them. The window letters were flat and indifferent, tired of carrying around boring old numbers. All they wanted was to lie on the hall rug and close their eyes. But this letter, it had a lot to say. It looked as if it was trying to keep from laughing or singing. The mole who lived under the rug came out and sniffed the letter, and the letter sniffed back.

Vega bent down and looked at it. The letter was covered in stickers of butterflies and flowers, and her own name was written in big red letters.

'Vega, is that you?'

Viola's voice was like a glass bell slicing through the walls. Vega hurried to hide the letter in her bag.

'I've made you sandwiches!'

Vega hated it when Viola cooked food for her. The food was always ice-cold even when Viola took it straight from the oven.

Viola came into the hall with a little plate of sandwiches.

Vega looked at the frosty cucumber and hard cheese. 'Thanks,' she said, 'but I'm not hungry.'

'Vega, don't be impolite when Viola has gone to such trouble for you.'

Dad stood in the doorway to the living room. Vega wasn't sure if he'd just arrived or if he'd been there all along. For some reason she hoped he hadn't seen her pick up Janna's letter.

'It doesn't matter,' said Viola, putting a hand on Vega's shoulder. Vega shuddered and took a step back without thinking.

'Vega!'

Dad's voice cracked like a whip. Vega rubbed her cheek.

'You'll say sorry to Viola! That's no way to behave.'

Vega looked down at the rug. She tried to raise her eyes to meet Viola's but couldn't. It was like looking into the horrible fluorescent lights at her father's office. Vega's eyes travelled up to Viola's throat where the silvery veins squirmed like white worms.

'Don't worry, Aaron,' said Viola with a light laugh that ran like a cold trickle down Vega's spine. 'I'll eat the sandwiches myself if Vega isn't hungry. Maybe you'd like to share one too?'

Dad reached out and took one. Vega watched in horror as he brought it to his mouth and took a big bite of the icy bread. It crunched as he chewed.

'Mm, good!' he said, looking at Viola with a smile full of frosty crumbs. His lips were completely blue, and with every bite the chill crept further up his face. He looked into Viola's eyes for several seconds without being blinded. Then he turned his gaze to Vega, and his eyes were brighter now, harder to look into.

'You should try one of Viola's sandwiches, Vega,' he said. 'You haven't eaten anything.'

He took and held the plate out to Vega. His face was white, almost like Viola's.

'Take one.'

Vega couldn't bear to look at Dad any longer. Her eyes drifted without her realising to Viola's. She was at once so dazzled she had to look down again. Blind spots danced in front of her eyes, a bit like woolly sheep.

'I... I have to do my homework,' she stammered, backing slowly down the hall to her room. Viola and Dad stood like statues with the plate of sandwiches held out as she closed the door.

She still had her shoes and coat on when she sank onto the bed. Dad was turning to ice under Viola's care, and Vega didn't know how to help him. The polar bears hidden under the cover eased off her coat and gave her a hug. Suddenly she heard rustling from her backpack. It sounded like a little animal whispering, trying to get out. Janna's letter! She opened the pack, and the letter flew into her hands. As she held it for a moment, it purred like a cat. It was soft and warm. And it was hers.

Hello Vega!
How are you? I'm fine.

You're really good at drawing! I thought the picture of the rhinoceros was beautiful, I hung it straight away by my bed in our caravan. Can you send me some more drawings?

I'm not so good at drawing but I usually sing with my mothers. Phoenix is especially good at singing, and Katja sings 'when the caravan requires', she says. I also like crosswords and watching the acrobats practise.

Yes, it's quite fun having two mothers. But I'd really like a brother or sister as well, or at least another kid to play with here at the circus. Maybe you can visit some time? We go to Kingstown next month. I'll look up when it is so maybe you can come and watch our show?

I'd also like to visit Giraffe Island sometime because I've never swum in the sea. Is it fun or dangerous? Do the pike and sharks nibble your toes off like my mum says? If you were a starfish you wouldn't need to worry, because if they lose an arm, they just grow a new one, even a whole new starfish. Freaky! Imagine growing a whole new person from your toe! Except then you'd have a twin, almost like having a brother or sister. Otherwise, it wouldn't be fun being a starfish because they have no brains.

I'm sending a picture of a duck in sunglasses that I ripped out of a magazine.

I hope you write again soon! I'm sending you our new address.

Regards,

Janna

Vega read the letter three times, as she'd done with Janna's first letter. She wished Janna could grow from her little toe like a twin, so they could be together all the time.

Vega decided not to tell her father. Janna was her secret. And she'd soon be coming to Kingstown on the mainland. Vega could run away to Janna's circus, escape from Viola and Dad, who was no longer her dad. She could stay there, away from the cold apartment. She could take all the animals, and maybe Hector as well, and just leave Giraffe Island.

Except that she couldn't. She couldn't leave Dad to freeze to death with Viola.

It had started raining outside, and the smell of cold wet leaves reached all the way up to the third floor. You could tell by the smell that they were changing from green to yellow and red.

Summer and warmth were disappearing, and so was Dad. She had to do something to get him back.

But what?

# 6

# The giraffe's tongue is blue

'I SEE, so it's no longer about a heart attack,' Hector said thoughtfully, breaking a stem from a swan plant and handing it to Vega. The flowers on the stem opened their wings and flew up in a small circle around Vega and Hector, then disappeared into the blue.

'No, I don't think it is,' said Vega. 'Dad has changed so much. You should see him; he looks all blue and white. I think he's freezing to death.'

'That doesn't sound very likely,' said Hector. 'People rarely freeze to death just like that. Unless there's an ice age, of course.'

It was always very slow walking around the garden with Hector because he insisted on taking his trolley, and it didn't roll easily over the grass. Sometimes Vega wondered if Hector might have trouble walking without it. He was pretty old. Though she didn't know how old. He didn't seem to know himself. 'Four hundred or forty, somewhere in between!' he would answer when she asked.

'This thing with your father is quite a mystery,' said Hector. 'You should probably engage a detective for this assignment. I could ask my agents if you like.'

'Maybe,' said Vega.

They'd passed the rock garden where the gnome plants grew. They looked like small red gnome hats poking up through the moss on top of the rocks. Vega had never seen a mature gnome plant because they grew very slowly. Hector said he'd planted them several years ago, but he thought they'd mature into fully fledged gnomes by the time Vega was ready to get her driving licence. Vega could hardly wait. She hoped the gnomes would be able to walk and run as soon as they appeared, so she could play with them. Maybe they could do somersaults or stand on their hands like small acrobats. This thought reminded her of Janna's letter.

'Guess what, Hector? I've got a friend who lives in a circus.'

Hector came to a sudden stop and began coughing violently. 'It must be the pollen from the liquorice perennials,' he sniffed. 'They flower every other week and I get allergies four times a year.'

He began walking again.

'Anyhow,' said Vega, 'her name is Janna and she's my pen

pal. She tours the world with a circus. Isn't that exciting?'

'Mm, a circus you say,' Hector mumbled, his eyes searching for something beyond the rock garden, beyond the treetops, beyond the clouds. 'What is it again, a circus... but what have we here?' he cried, stopping the trolley again.

Vega sighed. It seemed that Hector was suddenly as bad at listening as Dad.

He pointed towards the blueberry grove, where the bushes had grown several metres high and formed a grotto where you could sit and drink tea. Vega glimpsed something blue, in the middle of the grove, but too blue to be a blueberry. It was also too big, even if the blueberries here were as big as apples. The blue thing was crawling around making strange noises.

'What is it?' whispered Vega.

'Maybe the blueberries have all joined together to make a kind of live blueberry monster,' Hector whispered back. 'But it also resembles a bumbleboar. Or a pig monkey that's changed colour.'

Vega thought she could make out a few words from the creature. She stepped closer.

'Oohh! Yum yummy... fantastic! Wow... what a gold mine...'

It was hard to hear what the thing was saying, because it smacked loudly between words. It was moving between the blueberry bushes, standing on its hind legs, so it became very tall, taller than her.

'I think it's a person,' Vega whispered back to Hector.

'No, not a person!' said Hector. 'At best, a pallervant, but it's hard to determine at this distance. Careful, Vega, don't go any closer, it might bite!'

The blueberry bushes rustled, and out stepped the blue thing — not a blueberry monster, a bumbleboar, a pig monkey or a pallervant; it was an ordinary boy. Or not quite ordinary. He wore pale blue overalls too short for his long legs, and his face was almost entirely blue as well. He looked as if he'd been rolling in blueberries. The boy still had his mouth full, and he chomped as he spoke.

'Hi...yum...nice to...mmmmm...meet you.'

Hector picked up a stick from the ground, went over to the boy and poked him.

'Ow!' said the boy.

'Just as I thought,' said Hector. 'It could be a tinted moaner, but its head is a little too small... I think it's a bluenose.'

Vega examined the boy. His mouse-grey hair was tied in a little ponytail at the base of his neck, and his nose was wider than it was long. His eyes were set far apart. They were small slits with a hint of dark gleaming eyes, like coal-black marbles, the ones kids played with at school.

She recognised him. He was in the class next to hers. She'd seen him in the playground, where he was usually off by himself in a corner. Once she'd seen him lying beside an ant hill with a magnifying glass for the entire lunchtime.

'You're in Brig, aren't you?' she asked.

The boy nodded and swallowed the last of his mouthful. 'That's right! I'm Nelson.'

Nelson held his hand out to Vega. It was sticky.

'Vega. I'm in Schooner.'

'I know! You go around talking to yourself. Which is cool.'

Vega pulled back her hand and looked down.

'And you, old fella,' said Nelson holding out his hand to Hector. 'What's your name?'

'Blow me down with a feather!' said Hector. 'Fancy a bluenose greeting a perfectly normal person in the middle of his own garden. I'll have to report this.'

'He's called Hector,' said Vega. 'He's my grandfather.'

'Grandfather!' cried Nelson. 'Amazing! How does that work?'

'It works well,' said Vega.

'Do grandfathers always have these little trolleys and look so peculiar?'

'Yes, most do, I think.'

Nelson pulled a red notebook from one pocket in his overalls and a little pencil from another.

'Old men with lots of hair and small trolleys are called

grandfathers,' he muttered as he wrote. 'Excuse me, I just have to write down a few things while I remember them,' he said, continuing to write. 'The bigger the blueberry, the bluer it tastes...'

'What's that you're writing?' asked Hector. 'Where have you come from? Have they sent you to investigate me again? Since when did they start training bluenoses?'

'I haven't come from anywhere,' said Nelson. 'I just write down things I find interesting because I like collecting them. This garden has masses of interesting things to collect, did you know?'

'Of course I know,' snorted Hector. 'For example, I have the largest collection of gnome plants in the world!'

'Is that true?' asked Nelson. 'Can I see it? I have a whole chapter on gnomes here somewhere.' Nelson put the pencil between his teeth and flipped through his notebook. 'I try to keep some order in my categories, but there's so much to document,' he said apologetically.

'Is that so?' Hector sounded suspicious. 'May we hear some of it then? I've long been hunting for a reference work with something sensible to say.'

'Okay, let me see, here's a section about the colour blue.'

'Oh, my favourite!' said Hector. 'I know all about it, but let's hear.'

Nelson cleared his throat. 'Did you know that white cats with blue eyes are often deaf?' He looked up.

Hector nodded.

'And that the owl is the only creature that can see blue?'
Hector nodded.

'Did you know that mosquitos are more attracted to blue than to any other colour?'
Hector nodded.

'And that the sea's not really blue, but reflects the sky?'
Hector nodded.

'Did you know that the octopus has blue blood?'
Hector nodded.

'So, that's all I have,' said Nelson.

Vega couldn't believe her ears. How could Nelson know all that?

'You've forgotten the most important thing of all!' said Hector. 'Stretch out your tongue.'

Nelson stretched out his tongue, and it was entirely blue. 'Exactly! Just like the giraffe! Its tongue is blue. All the time, regardless of whether it's eaten blueberries or not. That's why the sea round Giraffe Island is blue. That bit about the sky, by the way, that's not really true. The sky is sometimes white and the sea doesn't go white, does it?'

Hector had an answer for everything. And it was quite true, Vega had never seen the sea around Giraffe Island turn white. Sometimes, too, the sky was red or gold, like at sunset, but the water in the sea didn't turn red or gold.

'What's more, the giraffe's tongue is very long, half a metre or more,' said Hector. 'It can scratch its ears with its tongue if it wants to.'

'Wow, that's the best fact I've had so far!' Nelson laughed and quickly wrote in his notebook: *The giraffe's tongue is very long and blue just like the sea around Giraffe Island.* The whole double page was covered in blue fingerprints.

'Otherwise, that sounds like an accurate collection of facts,' said Hector. 'You seem to be clever at finding out things, bluenose. Maybe you'd be interested in a little assignment Vega and I have taken up?'

At that moment, a car drove into the yard. Vega recognised it as belonging to one of Hector's agents.

'Ah, time for today's report!' said Hector.

An agent in a white coat hopped out of the car and came over. It was a woman with curly hair and glasses.

'Good afternoon, Hector, how are you?' she asked.

'Splendid!' said Hector. 'A lot going on as usual. And as you can see, I've just discovered a live bluenose which has grown up in my blueberry patch!'

The agent smiled with tight lips. 'I can see that. Have you eaten anything today?'

'Yes, of course. Come along and tell me what clues you've found. It's about time you showed up. I think you're a little behind in your reporting.'

The agent took Hector by the arm, and they began to walk slowly towards the house. Hector looked back over his shoulder and whispered urgently:

'Vega, you should ask bluenose if he can help you with

the Viola case. Code V. He seems a good detective. These agents aren't really to be trusted.'

The agent giggled but kept walking. They didn't seem very good, the agents. Vega wondered if they were really helping Hector with his investigations, or if they were just pretending.

'Well?' Nelson looked at Vega with narrowed eyes as if he expected her to say something. A frudbimble waggled about between them, but Nelson didn't seem to notice. Vega was suddenly nervous. She hardly ever talked to other children. No one at school ever asked her anything. What should she say?

'What's the investigation?' Nelson continued. His eyes shone as if it was Christmas and he was about to open a big present. 'Code V? What's that?'

'It's —' Vega looked around, hoping something would appear and stop Nelson from staring at her. Suddenly she saw it. A gigantic, golden-haired dog, standing still behind Nelson. It was so big it could look over Nelson's shoulder right at Vega. She couldn't understand how she'd missed it. Had it been there all along?

'Oh, sorry,' said Nelson. 'I forgot to introduce you! This is Flor.'

Vega couldn't believe her ears. Nelson could see the dog? Flor stepped from behind Nelson's back and towards Vega. She wagged her tail and pulled back her ears to show she was friendly. She'd kept as still as possible till Nelson had introduced her so she wouldn't scare the girl. But Vega wasn't afraid. As Flor took a few steps forward, Vega put out a hand to pat her on the head. Then she threw her arms around her.

'Isn't she beautiful?' said Nelson.

'Yes.' Vega buried her face in Flor's fur. 'She's absolutely wonderful.'

'So . . . Code V? The assignment?' asked Nelson again when Vega had released Flor. 'It seems to be very important. I'm good at listening to very important things. At least if they're not boring.'

Vega squirmed. 'We can talk about it later, maybe,' she said. She had to find a way to distract Nelson. She plucked up courage. 'I know a place I think you'll like. We can go there if you want. It's Hector's Paraphernalium.'

'His parapher-whatsit?'

'His Paraphernalium. It's his garage.'

# 7

# Hamsters can carry half their body weight in their cheeks

HECTOR'S PARAPHERNALIUM, as he called it, was very like any other garage. There were things everywhere. On shelves, in boxes, on the floor. The difference was that Hector's things were much more interesting to rummage through. Every time Vega went in, she found something new and exciting, and when she showed the thing to Hector, he always had a fantastic story to tell her about it. Or else he'd never seen it before in his life.

The door creaked. Vega went first, then Nelson and finally Flor. The first thing Flor did was sneeze so hard her nose hit the floor. Dust spun round in the light streaming from the open door. Vega stepped onto a stool and pulled a string hanging from the ceiling, and the lights came on.

The Paraphernalium was very big. There were several different rooms and sections, all filled to the brim with things, stuff, other things, rubble and junk. Vega didn't know how big it really was because you couldn't explore everything at once. And every time she went in, the rooms were in slightly different places.

Just inside the front door stood something that looked like a car. Vega had seen it many times. It was one of the few things in the Paraphernalium that was always in the same place. It was no ordinary car, however. It had four wheels and a steering wheel, but that's where the similarities ended. Hector had built his car from parts he'd found in the abandoned cake factory, the one right next to the toothpaste factory where Nelson lived. Hector had picked up dough machines and sprinkle choppers and icing spreaders and transformed them into carburettors, gearboxes and washers. He called it the Muffinmobile.

Vega had never seen the Muffinmobile running; it had sat in the Paraphernalium gathering dust for as long as she could remember. Hector said it worked fine, and that he was just waiting for the right moment to take it out for a little spin.

'Wow!' cried Nelson, running past the Muffinmobile to a shelf of old radios. 'These are cool! Do they work?' He began pushing and turning all the knobs, but no sound came. 'My mother would love these! Her favourite thing is listening to the radio!'

Vega smiled a little. She wondered if her mother also liked listening to the radio.

'Hector says he took them all apart to build one big super radio. He has a lot of different assignments to keep track of, and with a super radio he can tune in to frequencies from agents all over the world.'

'That's exciting!' Nelson fished out his notebook and scribbled something down. He'd barely finished before he looked up and saw something else. 'Look at this!'

Nelson ran to a box filled with bits of old plumbing. He dug out a funnel and put it on his head. 'What do you think?'

Vega laughed. 'Nice! You should wear it!'

Flor, who'd followed Nelson, looked up from the box. Her nose was stuck in a pipe. She wasn't really made for the Paraphernalium. She nudged Nelson's leg to signal that they should leave. But Nelson had made a new discovery: an old gramophone with two funnels, one silver and one gold.

'That's so Hector can listen to hidden messages on old records,' said Vega. 'He's listened to all the operas in the world. The gold funnel plays them normally, but the silver one plays them backwards. That's how he can hear if there's any secret information hidden in the music.'

'Has he found any?' asked Nelson.

'No, he likes opera so much he listens to the gold funnel.'

Vega went to the shelf with pieces of old toys. There

were parts of dolls, old teddy bears, radio-controlled cars and worn-out wooden blocks. She blew dust from a small sparkly box and opened the lid. A melody started playing while a little ballerina rose from the box and began to pirouette. Vega laughed.

'Wait, can you do that again?' Nelson asked, standing beside her.

'What?'

Nelson dug in his overalls pocket. He fished out a little tape recorder, pushed a button and spoke into it:

'Laugh number thirty-three.'

Then he pointed the tape recorder at Vega and looked at her expectantly. Vega hadn't even noticed she'd laughed. She tried to do it again, but it sounded false.

'Uh.' Nelson turned it off. 'I'll try to catch it sometime when you're not aware. It'll be perfect for my collection.'

Nelson wandered between boxes and shelves to a little corridor that led to a couple of other rooms. Flor couldn't fit in the corridor, so she joined Vega, who was still looking at the toys. Vega had never seen them before, even though she'd been in the Paraphernalium a hundred times. Who had played with them? Were they her mother's old toys? In her imagination, the paper doll sat down and began building a high tower of wooden blocks.

She heard Nelson call from another room: 'Come here, Vega! You have to see this!'

Nelson had squeezed in between some old bikes and

had made a path to a small cupboard Vega had never seen before.

'Your grandfather's like a hamster!' he cried with his head halfway in a box. 'He collects everything! Did you know hamsters can carry half their body weight in their cheeks?'

Vega didn't know.

She squeezed over to the cupboard Nelson had found. He'd opened drawers and pulled things off the shelves. Juggling rings, feather boas, sparkling jackets, coat rings and funny hats.

'This is perfect! We can have a masquerade!'

Nelson flung a pink feather boa round his neck and pulled a puffy white skirt up over his overalls, just like the one the ballerina in the little box wore.

Vega looked at all the things. They sparkled and shone with glitter and sequins. It was as if they'd opened a door to a...

'Wow!' Nelson gasped. He'd pulled down a box, and behind it was an enormous poster leaning against the wall. The colours had faded but you could still make out the picture. A man in a green coat and top hat, with lots of curly hair, carrying a baton. He had a wide smile and the wrinkles round his eyes formed perfect sunflowers. He stood in the middle of a circus ring backed by red curtains, and two horses reared, one on each side of him, with glittering plumes between their ears. Above the circus director's head, big gold letters read:

'Circus Hectoramus,' the children said in unison.

There was no doubt about it. The hair was darker, the smile whiter, the posture straighter, but the circus director on the poster was without doubt Vega's grandfather.

They heard the door squeak.

'Figment of my imagination! Bluenose! What are you up to?' It was Hector's voice.

'Just looking!' Vega called back, signalling to Nelson to be quiet. 'We'll be out soon!'

'Shouldn't we ask him about the poster?' Nelson whispered.

'No, don't say anything,' said Vega.

She didn't know why, but she had a feeling she wouldn't ask Hector about this. Not yet. It was too strange. Hector had behaved so oddly when she told him about Janna and the circus, as if he didn't want to talk about it. He'd never said anything about a circus. But here was this poster, and the green coat. It looked like the coat Vega's mother was wearing in the picture. Circus Hectoramus. Janna, who lived in a circus. Was that just coincidence? Vega's head whirled. She had to find out everything she could before she asked Hector anything.

'Okay. Are you ready?' she said quietly to Nelson.

He nodded. He looked quite funny in his blue overalls, with the pink boa and ballerina skirt and a face stained with blueberries.

'Absolutely. Ready for what?'

'You have to help me figure something out,' she said.

Nelson's narrow eyes narrowed even further. 'Code V?' he whispered back.

'Yes, among other things. And a bit more. I don't understand it myself. First, I have to tell you a few things. But not here, not now.'

'Oh, is it because it's an... enigma?' asked Nelson, his eyes bright as stars.

'Exactly,' said Vega. 'It's an enigma.'

# Polar bears are lefthanded

'BUT HOW SHALL I ASK?'

'Just straight out! What's the name of your circus? It's not hard.'

'But shouldn't I explain why I want to know? It's not something you ask just like that.'

'Of course it is! I ask people things all the time. What's your name? What's your grandfather's name? What's a grandfather? Can I pat your hair? People don't think it's strange. "What's the name of your circus?" is a perfectly normal question. And we have to know!'

Nelson and Flor walked with Vega almost all the way home from Hector's house. Vega hadn't even noticed, because they'd been talking the whole way down the mountain, past the reservoir and the harbour and all the way to Vega's street. She told him all about Viola, about the icy sandwiches, how the apartment had turned frosty and how her father had changed. Then she told him everything about her mother, how she'd never known anything about her and that the only picture of her was the old photo on Hector's wood stove, where she was wearing the green coat and the top hat just like Hector in the Circus Hectoramus poster.

Then she told him about Janna, how she'd got her as a pen pal and that she lived in a circus and that Hector had behaved strangely when he heard. Nelson half-ran beside her, writing everything he could in his notebook.

'Oh wow,' he puffed, 'this is a bigger mystery than I could have dreamed up! The pen pal I got at Fun Hour is called Lars and he lives in a terrace house. He likes stamp collecting and chewing gum, that's all he's come up with.'

Nelson had quickly realised that they had to find out the name of Janna's circus before they jumped to conclusions. It was unlikely to be Circus Hectoramus, which would be too big a coincidence. Vega took Janna's letter from her backpack and let Nelson read it, but he found no clues about the name of the circus.

They sat on a bench in the sun a block from Vega's house. Flor lay down in front so the children could rest their tired feet on her back.

'We can't go in,' said Vega. 'If everything was normal, we could have, and Dad would have made us sandwiches. But I don't dare take you in. She might be there.'

'Of course.' Nelson gave a shrug. 'We can't discuss the mystery in the apartment with the mystery elephant! Even if it would be interesting to see the ice queen up close. Maybe I could take a sample of her ice to investigate. But we can do that later! First, we must ask Janna about her circus! Then I'll go home and think about the rest.'

Vega smiled at him. Everything was happening so quickly. But Nelson seemed to be a good detective. And Hector had just said they should hire one.

Vega took her geography workbook from her backpack, and the pencil case with all the different coloured pens. She turned to an empty page in the book and chose a light green felt-tip. She would have liked to write to Janna on nicer paper, but the workbook would have to do.

Hi Janna!

How are you? I'm fine. Thanks for your letter! It was really fun to read. And it's great that you liked my drawing. I've got lots more drawings if you want to see them.

'What's that, what drawing?'

Nelson was leaning over Vega's shoulder, curious to see what she was writing.

'I sent her a drawing of a rhinoceros in my first letter.'

'Oh! Can you draw?'

'No, not really, I just doodle a bit.'

'Can I see?'

Vega took out her sketchbook. She'd never shown it to anyone. Not even Hector had seen it. But there was something about Nelson that made Vega want to tell him everything. He was like a hungry puppy, pouncing on everything and gobbling it up. Like a waterfall that never stopped. He never frowned when she explained something, like the other children at school. And there were no clouds above his head either.

Nelson opened Vega's sketchbook and began flipping through pages. There were the crossing-zebras that helped her over the road, the asphalt beavers who lived under the pavement, the grizzly bear from the shower, the stone lions from the mountain, the little woolly mammoth from the wardrobe, the spoonlurks, the fasterers, the fourfentipedes and all the other animals from Hector's garden.

'Vega, these are fantastic,' said Nelson, flipping more pages. 'How can you make all these up?'

'They're not made up,' said Vega. 'I just draw what I see. Look, these polar bears have moved into my room since Viola started living with us.'

Nelson laughed.

'And what's this?' He touched the page where Vega had drawn a strange creature that stood on two legs with a long trunk wound around its body.

'That's a trunktoothed rumpling.' Vega laughed. 'It lives in Hector's garden.'

'Wow! Oh, I'll have to come and see it!'

'Of course,' said Vega. 'Though it can be hard to find. Hector normally chases it away with a broom because it eats up all his perch plants.'

While Nelson looked through her sketchbook, Vega carried on writing her letter to Janna.

Today I visited my grandfather and played in his Paraphernalium. Do you have a grandfather? Or a Paraphernalium? I also met a dog called Flor which is almost as big as a horse. Do you have horses at the circus? Or dogs?

I'd love to see you at the circus when you come to the Mainland. I don't know if I can, because Dad has been very busy lately and I don't think he'll let me go alone. The ferries between Giraffe Island and the mainland are huge, like floating towns where you can easily get lost. I heard they have shops full of sweets, but I don't know if it's true because I've never been on one.

Have you ever been on a ferry? Or do you normally take all your circus animals on the train or the bus? By the way, what is the name of your circus? Just wondering.

Auf Wiedersehen,

Vega

'You write with your left hand!' said Nelson when she'd finished. He'd put the sketchbook away and was looking over her shoulder again.

'Did you know that polar bears are lefthanded?'

Vega shook her head.

'It's true. It's in *Nelson's Interesting Facts*. They're also the biggest carnivores living on land. Maybe not including the ones in your bedroom. Can we send your polar bear drawing to Janna?'

Vega tore the letter from the geography book, then looked for the polar bear drawing in her sketchbook and tore that out too. Then she folded them and taped the sides together, and on the front she wrote the address Janna had sent. She realised she'd broken Ms Hum's rule that all letters should be corrected by her before they were posted. 'No cheating!' she'd said. But Vega had the feeling that if Ms Hum knew the circumstances she would understand.

'Come on,' said Nelson, 'let's go and post it!'

# A leech has thirty-two brains

THE DAYS THAT FOLLOWED, while Vega waited for a reply from Janna, were long and syrupy. Not the good sort of syrup that Hector put in his tea, but a dark, treacly substance that lay and clogged things up so it was hard to move, hard to think.

Vega and Nelson had begun meeting outside in the schoolyard during breaks. Since they'd posted the letter to Janna, Nelson had been intent on solving Vega's mystery. He'd even found his old magnifying glass and got himself a new notebook, a little bigger than the old one. He'd written NELSON'S MYSTERIES AND SUCH in big letters on its green cover. Inside, he'd drawn a kind of map of the mystery. He'd drawn lines between various names and words, had drawn pictures and graphs and written out equations. Every break he asked Vega questions that might lead to clues. He interviewed her about Viola: how she behaved, in what way she was cold and if she was colder in the day or at night, whether it made a difference how close you stood to her, and if Vega's father ever complained that he was freezing.

'No, Dad doesn't notice anything,' said Vega. 'He's in her grasp, she's bewitched him. Frozen him.'

'Right, right,' said Nelson, writing in his book. He'd taped small bits of ice to the page around Viola's name. They'd melted, of course, but it gave a sense of the theme, he said. He'd drawn a line from Viola's name to a circle where he'd written *Dad*. What was he like before? Was he warm or cold to begin with? Hard or soft? Wet or dry? Like a sponge? Or a pinecone? Or a brick?

'I don't know,' said Vega. 'Dad was just . . . like Dad.' She thought of the clouds sailing above his head, and his heart, swelling big and blue.

'He was neither warm nor cold. He was like . . . like ordinary water.'

'Aha! Like water!' Nelson hurried to draw circles and arrows and squiggles on the map. 'Of course the question arises of whether he's like tap water, salt water, aquarium water and so on, but we can look into that later. So, if Viola, or Code V, is equal to ice, it's clear that your dad, who is equal to water, also freezes, because that's what happens to water when it's cold enough. So, we just need something warm, or x in our calculation, to save your father from freezing!'

'Yes, but what could that be?

'I don't know. Fire, maybe?

'We can't start a fire in our apartment.'

'Maybe not. Hm... Oh to be a leech at a time like this! Do you know they have thirty-two brains? They use thirty to look for food and only two to ponder the mysteries of life. But if it was me, I'd use all thirty-two brains at once to solve this mystery! Or maybe I'd save one to learn more about ants. I'm missing some facts about ants.'

Vega giggled when she thought how big Nelson's head would have to be to hold thirty-two brains. He would look really silly.

'We need an x factor!' Nelson continued. 'Something warm. It's a long time till next summer, so we can't wait for that. Maybe we could trick him into a sauna?'

Before Viola, Vega used to go to the Giraffe Baths with her father. Dad couldn't draw a chalk circle there, so Vega's animals splashed freely in the water. She rode sea pigs and played with bear seals till Dad's eyebrows ran into the chlorinated water, and he took her to the sauna. It was quiet there. Only a few desert marmots sat grumbling in a corner, but they mostly wanted to be left in peace.

'It could work,' she said.

'Or,' continued Nelson, 'is there a very warm person you could take home with you?'

'I don't know.'

'What was your mother like? Warm, cold? Dry, wet? Hard, soft? Like a pinecone or a sponge?'

'I don't know much about her. Hector sometimes says she was fiery. But I think he means her mood. Sometimes I think she might have been a dragon of some kind.'

The paper doll in Vega's head puffed out smoke.

'Perfect! Fiery! That's our factor x. It's her. So, if we could find your mother, I think we'd have our answer!'

Nelson enthusiastically circled various words in his notebook. Fire, water, ice, snow, pinecone, dragon. Numbers and symbols.

'But...that's impossible,' said Vega. She wasn't prepared for this. 'No one knows where she is. Not even Hector.'

'Are you sure about that? I haven't finished the calculation with the circus yet. What if she's still at Circus Hectoramus?'

'Why would she be? Maybe she's never even been at a circus. We only saw Hector on the poster.'

'But isn't this *grandfather* your mother's father? It sounds like they're related anyway...'

More symbols and numbers were circled in Nelson's notebook. Then he gasped and widened his black marble eyes.

'Didn't you say there was a picture of her at Hector's

house? What if that's from the circus? There might be something in the background.'

Nelson insisted they go back to Hector's to investigate further, maybe use the super radio, or play an old record backwards, or at least ask him about it all. But Vega didn't want to. If Hector had wanted to talk about Circus Hectoramus, he would have. He usually told Vega everything. Why didn't he want to talk about the circus?

Thoughts whirled in Vega's head and none of them belonged. However hard she tried, she couldn't put the pieces together. Had Hector really been a circus director? Did that mean that Vega's mother had grown up in a circus, just like Janna? And what if it was the same circus where Janna lived? It was unlikely, but you couldn't rule anything out, as Nelson said. And why had this come out now, right when Viola had appeared and her father was starting to freeze? Everything had been fine till Viola came into their lives. The elephant in her father's china shop. In his heart.

'Okay, maybe we can't go further with our investigation till we hear back from Janna,' said Nelson. 'That will give us a new clue so we can think about what to do next.'


IT HAD BEEN a week since they sent the last letter to Janna. Viola was at their house almost every day now. The chill in the apartment grew deeper and denser. The ice had spread outside the apartment, to the stairwell, over the whole courtyard. The leaves in the treetops were red and yellow like fire, but they still couldn't melt the frost creeping up their trunks. Vega saw through her binoculars that frost had started to creep out from the beaches over the sea around Giraffe's Head, and that the dolphins and mermaids had fled in terror.

The white car with the shifty eyes had covered the whole street with a thin layer of ice, and the crossing-zebras slid about with chattering teeth. They hadn't had time to grow winter fur with the sudden change in weather.

It was Friday and Ms Hum said she couldn't think of anything fun to do in the Fun Hour so they might as well go home. It didn't matter to Vega. She couldn't have had fun today anyway.

Vega went up the snowy steps and put the key in the door to the apartment. She couldn't turn it. The lock was frozen solid.

Vega knocked at the door. She heard her father's voice. 'Coming!'

The voice sounded as if it came from far away, as if he were coming from down a long corridor. The door handle was pushed down, but Dad had to coax it back and forth a few times till the ice gave way. Snow lay in drifts in the hall.

'Hello Vega,' he said, and his voice sounded deep-frozen. His eyes were pale and looked right through Vega. 'Come in, sweetie, how are things?' Ordinary words that sounded like Dad, but it wasn't Dad.

Vega stepped inside. Iceblocks lined the hallway. Big blocks stacked on top of each other, blocking the doors into the living room and Dad's bedroom. They looked like boxes.

'Vega, we have something to tell you,' said Dad in his frozen voice, crouching down in front of her. The ice on his trousers crackled as he bent his knees. 'Viola, come here!'

The blocks of ice moved, and Viola stepped into the hall. She looked taller, almost to the ceiling, her hair jet-black like a veil down her back. She came over to Vega's father and put her arms around him. She looked into his eyes, and Vega could suddenly see how her father's big, surging heart stopped and the surface became crystal clear and coated in ice. He looked small in Viola's arms, as if he was shrinking, stiffening. Freezing.

'Vega, we have some news,' said Dad. 'We've decided that since Viola is already living with us most of the time, she might as well bring all her things here. Move in, in fact.' Viola and Dad looked at each other again and smiled. The ice grew thicker around Dad's heart. 'We'll be a little cramped to start with, but after a bit, we might find a small house somewhere that will hold all three of us. What do you think of that, Vega?'

Everything stopped.

The kitchen clock fell silent.

The trees in the street outside stopped sighing.

All the cars in the whole town stood still.

The clouds in the sky stopped floating and hung like dead puppets from their strings.

Vega's heart fell from the top of a cliff somewhere inside her and tumbled down like an autumn leaf.

Dad and Viola wore frozen smiles in a frozen embrace, as if in a photograph. Their empty eyes looked straight ahead. Time had stopped and Vega didn't know if it ever would start again. She looked around the snowy apartment for a frozen second that felt endless. A polar bear cub had hidden among the iceblocks, and a snow hare was pressed to the wall. Vega didn't know if they were petrified like her.

She took two more steps into the apartment, past Dad and Viola. They didn't move. It was like stepping into a snowy postcard. One like the ones Vega and Dad used to send at Christmas time, where Vega was in her father's arms on a sledge coming down the hill, with the text *Merry Christmas and Happy New Year* in gold letters above them. There was a card like that taped to the fridge. Vega went into the kitchen.

Snowflakes hovered in mid-air. She moved between them to the fridge. There was the card: *Merry Christmas and Happy New Year from Vega and her Dad*. Vega was only five in the picture. Her woolly hat was over her eyes, and she was laughing, her mouth wide. Dad had a red nose and snow inside his jacket and his big heart was blue and warm even though they were sitting on the snowy sledging hill.

Vega took the card from the fridge and tucked it inside her jacket.

She was about to zigzag between the snowflakes back to the hall when she saw it. In the middle of the dining table, which was covered in several centimetres of fallen snow, was a small, melted patch, as if someone had put a cup of hot tea on the table. And there lay a letter. It didn't jump or jiggle as the last letter had. It lay almost completely still, gasping for air. Janna's letter. Vega wondered how many hours it had lain there. She snatched it to her, under her jacket and close to her heart so it could warm up. Then she went right through the unmoving snowflakes in the kitchen, and along the hall past the deep-frozen Dad and Viola. Closing the door carefully behind her, she went down the steps and onto the street.

Once outside, she ran. Faster and faster, till the wind in her ears told her that time had started again. A car tooted and stopped with a screech right in front of her. The frozen second had passed, the clouds floated on, and Dad and Viola had likely got up and were wondering where she'd gone. She had to get away quickly, before they came after her. But where should she go?

As Vega ran, the letter inside her jacket came to life and began to beat, faster and faster, keeping time with her own heart.

# 10

## Worms are blind but can tell light from dark

VEGA HAD NEVER BEEN on this side of town before. Normally she wouldn't dare come here alone, but these weren't normal circumstances. The dirt road snaked between rubbish bins and rickety fences. Sometimes it was hard to tell where the road was, because the grass had grown over it and brown leaves were scattered everywhere. Vega went on running in what she hoped was the right direction. Old brick and concrete buildings looked at her dully. Abandoned for so long, they had given up trying to look welcoming. There was nobody to be seen. And no animals either. Vega didn't usually feel lonely like this when she was alone.

Nelson had said that he lived in the factory part of town. But how would she know which building? And was he even at home? Should she knock on all the factory doors one by one till she found the right one? She looked up at the sky. It was coloured with the pink-grey light you sometimes get in the autumn, a light that tricks you into thinking the sun will soon go down even though it's hours until bedtime.

At the same moment she heard a bark and just managed to turn before something big and hairy threw itself at her and knocked her to the ground. For a second Vega thought it was the grizzly bear from her shower that had run away from the chill of the apartment. But of course, it was Flor.

'Flor, you gave me a fright!'

The dog looked at her with friendly eyes. Her tail wagged, rocking her big body from side to side. She gently grabbed Vega's jacket in her teeth and helped her to her feet. Then she nudged Vega with her nose towards her own back and Vega climbed up. Her fur was warm and soft. Flor began to run. She veered off the path and went through a thicket, crawled through a hole in a fence and padded to an open door in one of the buildings. She signalled to Vega to hold on tight, and Vega buried her fingers in the dog's fur and clung to her back. It was dark inside the building and Vega couldn't see a thing. Suddenly Flor was climbing a staircase. Up higher and higher, in a long spiral. At the top of the stairs was a door. Flor nudged it with her nose and went in.

They came directly into a warm kitchen. The sink was full of dirty dishes, and on the kitchen table was an ashtray overflowing with cigarette butts.

'Vega! You came just at the right time!'

Nelson ran into the kitchen. He was wearing his blue overalls even though he was indoors. Nelson didn't seem to find it at all strange that Vega had ridden in on Flor in broad daylight, without ever visiting him before, and without being invited. Flor lay down on the floor and Vega crawled from her back.

'Thank you, Flor,' said Vega. 'Nelson,' she said, 'a terrible thing has happened. Viola is moving in with us. Everything is covered in snow and Dad is freezing to death. We have to do something!'

'Wow! Then things are hotting up although we haven't even lit a fire!' Nelson said eagerly. 'Have you had an answer from Janna?'

Vega pulled out the letter. Nelson grabbed and opened it.

'This is so exciting, I can't wait!' Then he paused. 'Sorry, it's your letter. Here. You read it first.'

He passed the letter to Vega and she unfolded it. The notepaper had small kittens printed on the bottom corner. She took a deep breath.

Hi Vega,

How are you? I'm fine. Thanks for your letter! Your drawing of the polar bears was really good. We don't have any polar bears here at the circus. I've heard they can be very dangerous. But we have many other animals, Phoenix looks after them and decides which will be in which performance. My favourites are the ponies. They're so small they can jump through hoops high in the air and do flips on the way down. I usually feed them four-leaf clovers outside the tent before the show. That gives them extra luck when they're doing their difficult tricks.

Katja says it's just a superstition. Then Phoenix says she's a dry ball. Mothers!

How fantastic that you've met a dog as big as a horse. That might mean it's the same size as one of our ponies: big for a dog and small for a horse.

I've never been on a ferry either, but I hope to one day. I think it would be hard to fit all our circus wagons on board. It's easiest for us to travel on land. And soon we'll be in Kingstown! Will you come and watch? You could come without your father, or maybe bring your grandfather? We'll be putting our tent up in Keytree Park. I'm sending a programme with this letter. We're called Circus Rumbunctus.

I have to go now; Mum's going to practise singing before the performance and I have to help with the animals.

Hope to see you soon!

Best wishes from Janna

Vega slumped onto a kitchen chair.

'Is it not the same circus? Circus Hectoramus?' asked Nelson.

She shook her head.

'Oh bother! I'd almost solved it.'

It would have been too good to be true. The little spark of hope that had been lit inside Vega when she found the poster at Hector's house went out as if someone had shovelled snow onto a candle. It probably hadn't been likely that Vega's mother would be at Janna's circus, even if it had been Circus Hectoramus. But it had been something to hold onto, a thread. A fire to warm Dad. If her mother really was fiery. Or if she even existed. Vega had never needed a mother, didn't know what a mother would give her that a father couldn't. But suddenly it was imperative that they find her mother. But what if Dad's water and her mother's fire didn't mix? What if fire and water just became... smoke?

Nelson had taken out his magnifying glass to examine Janna's letter. He also unfolded the programme Janna had included with the letter.

It was warm and stuffy in the little kitchen. Vega couldn't breathe. She took off her jacket and threw it on the floor. Flor picked it up at once and hung it on the back of a chair. Nelson looked up and his gaze landed on Vega's arm.

'That's a cool birthmark.'

Vega instinctively put her hand on her arm. No one had ever commented on her birthmark before. She looked down at the little giraffe. It was actually quite cute.

'Hmm, clues, clues...' Nelson mumbled, looking at the programme again. He moved the magnifying glass over every centimetre. It was colourful, full of stars and fireworks. In the middle was a picture of a fat lady in a top hat and green dress. She held her arms outstretched as if she wanted to hug everyone in sight. She smiled widely with red lips that seemed to almost bulge from the page. Above her head were the words CIRCUS RUMBUNCTUS in big gold letters. Beneath her, in smaller letters, it said:

Welcome to a fantastic show of acrobats, tightrope walkers, clowns, fire-eaters and unusual animals! Join me, Katja Rumbuc, on a journey you'll never forget, through a world you never knew existed!

'Wait a minute,' Nelson muttered. 'Who is this Katja Rumbuc?'

Katja. The circus director.

'It must be Janna's mother,' said Vega. 'She said that one of her mothers is a circus director and she's called Katja.'

'Aha! A *mother*.' Nelson held the picture next to Vega's face and looked intently between the two.

'Well, the resemblance is not immediately obvious... But it's not completely out of the question.'

'What?'

'What if this is your mother?'

'Katja?'

'Well, why not? It could be her. You have to trust your instincts sometimes. Like a worm. Did you know that worms are blind but can still tell the difference between light and dark? I call that trusting your gut. I think I may have a bit of worm in me, maybe not in my guts but in my genes, because I always trust my instincts. Maybe one of my ancestors was a worm. Or maybe one of my parents is a worm without telling me. Worms are fantastic creatures.'

Vega looked at the lady. She wore a green dress covered in sequins that accentuated her full figure, and a black feather boa round her neck. Her curly red hair flowed from under her top hat like lava from a volcano. Her face had green eyeshadow all the way up to her eyebrows. She was a little too glamorous. She didn't look at all the way Vega imagined her mother. Admittedly she had curly hair like Vega, but any likeness ended there. And Vega felt nothing when she looked at her. No beating heart, like with Janna's letter. Surely she'd recognise her own mother?

The paper doll nearby painted her lids in green eyeshadow and looked sceptical.

'Katja Rumbuc... Circus Rumbunctus,' said Nelson. 'What if... what if they change the name of the circus when they get a new director? This circus could have been called Circus Hectoramus when Hector was director.'

All the hope that Vega had just lost came rushing back in a flood.

'At least, when you think about it,' Nelson continued, 'it's quite logical. Rumbuc —Rumbunctus Hector — *Hectoramus*. If someone called Milli was the circus director, it might be called *Circus Millimetre*. Look, this Katja even has the same hat that Hector wore in the poster, or at least it looks very similar. And even if this isn't your mother, maybe your mother lives at the circus? If Hector once lived there. Or maybe there's someone there who knows who she is and where she's gone? We can't be sure of anything, but this is our best clue. Besides, my gut tells me we should check it out. And you know that I'm basically half worm, so my gut is never wrong.'

Vega looked at Nelson. Hiring him as a detective was the best thing she'd ever done.

'We have to go to the circus,' she said. 'And we have to go now.'

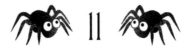

# Spiders have transparent blood

FLOR WOULDN'T LET NELSON ride on her back anymore. It had been practical a few years ago when he was smaller, and frankly the only way to get him to school on time. If she let him go by himself, he'd stop and look at tiny ants or count the bees in a beehive. But these last years he'd grown, shot up so high that Flor had to stand on a chair to brush his hair. His blue overalls would soon be too small; they already stopped halfway up his legs, leaving his ankles bare. And if he sat on her back, his feet dragged on the ground. So usually Flor went behind and nudged him in the back to try and keep him going straight ahead, not stopping all the time.

But this was no ordinary day. There was no time to waste, you could feel it. Flor had filled a little backpack with sandwiches and toothbrushes while the children sat in the kitchen talking. In case.

The smell of adventure was strong in the air.

Nelson pulled his knees up as high as he could and buried his fingers in the fur of Flor's neck.

'Hold on!' he called back to Vega, who hugged him around the waist. Flor set off at a gallop. 'Flor, run to Lotsberget! Quick as you can!'

Flor ran straight through the hole in the fence, followed the dirt road a little way and then turned off into the forest. She kept to the smaller paths. If people were already a little frightened of her, it would be nothing compared to seeing her galloping along with two children on her back.


WHEN THEY REACHED Hector's garden, Flor dropped panting to the ground.

'Come on, Flor! We can't stop!' cried Nelson, running to the house.

The air was damp, so Hector's house was swelling into a palace. It was always confusing when this happened. Doors and windows never ended up in the same place as before, so Nelson and Vega had to run around the house to find the door, which was now a five-metre-high gate. Vega ran up the steep stairs and was about to knock on the door when they heard a car in the driveway. A cold wind swept over the stairs.

'Oh no,' said Vega. 'It's Dad's car! It's Dad and Viola! They've followed us here!'

Vega and Nelson rushed around to the back of the house with Flor on their heels. It was lucky that Hector never locked the doors. The Paraphernalium was open, and they managed to slip in just as the car pulled up.

They heard the car doors slam and quick feet on gravel. Vega and Nelson hid behind a shelf of pots, while Flor made herself as small as she could behind a statue of a sabre-toothed tiger. Vega signalled to the others to be quiet.

'What's going on?'

That was Hector's voice, right outside the door to the Paraphernalium. He must have been in the garden without them noticing.

'Hector, have you seen Vega?'

Dad's voice sounded worried and full of rain. Or snow.

The steps came closer.

'No, I haven't seen her today,' said Hector, pushing his trolley right up to the Paraphernalium door. 'Has she gone up in smoke?'

A butterfly found its way in through the door opening and landed on Flor's nose. Vega saw that it was a spotty peacock butterfly. The dots on its wings worked as eyes. Excellent spies, Hector would say. Flor looked cross-eyed at the butterfly, and the butterfly looked back with all its eyes. Flor's nose wrinkled and she gasped for breath.

'No!' Nelson hissed. 'She's going to sneeze!'

Flor gasped again and her eyes filled with tears. Then the butterfly flapped its wings and flew back out the doorway.

Flor and the children sighed in relief.

'She's run away from home,' Dad said from in the garden. 'I thought she must have come here.'

'No, she hasn't been here for a long time,' said Hector after a moment's silence. He looked in through the doorway. Vega met her grandfather's gaze. She held her breath and put her finger to her lips. Hector's eyes sparkled.

'No, I have no idea where she could be,' Hector continued, pushing his trolley closer to the door so it blocked their view. 'This is true. And you know how I am, transparent as a spider! Couldn't lie if I tried! Did you know that spiders have transparent blood? Well, they do. They can't hold anything in: secrets flow in through their ears and run straight out of their mouths!'

'That's amazing!' Nelson took out his notebook of interesting facts and whispered as he wrote: 'Spiders have transparent blood...'

'Shh!' Vega whispered.

Flor put her paw gently to Nelson's mouth. Hector started coughing violently outside.

'My lungs are terrible!' Hector slapped his chest. 'It must be the old dragon candy I found in my pantry. When it's too old it can make you cough smoke. Watch out now that I don't start spewing fire.'

Vega smiled at the thought of Hector's dragon sweets that he kept in a box at the back of his pantry. They were just bits of hay and syrup wrapped in baking paper. He often talked about going dragon hunting, but he never quite got around to it.

She heard Dad mumbling something outside the door.

'I think she has a new friend,' said Hector. 'A bluenose, lives somewhere in the forest. My best tip is to look there!'

'Okay,' said Dad. 'Thanks anyway, Hector!'

They heard the car doors slam and the engine start, the tyres rolling down the drive. When it had gone, the door to the Paraphernalium opened with a creak.

'Well I never, I have ghosts in my Paraphernalium.' Hector looked at the children with a small smile. 'The question is whether they are as transparent as spiders.'

'HECTOR,' SAID VEGA. 'You must help us escape. We have to leave Giraffe Island and go to the Mainland. Right now. We can catch the ferry if we hurry.'

'Oh! I thought I smelled adventure on you. Has something happened that I should know about?'

Vega and Nelson looked at each other.

'No,' said Nelson. 'But we need a driver. And a car, ideally.'

'I have a car at least!' said Hector. 'The Muffinmobile never fails!'

Vega looked into the corner where the Muffinmobile stood. Dust bunnies peeped in surprise from the bonnet.

'But... are you sure it still works?' she asked.

'Works?? That's the least of it! It drives smooth as butter, purrs like a cat, rolls like a bun!'

'When did you last use it?'

'Now let me see. It was a while ago. Maybe a few years. Or more. But that doesn't mean a thing in the world of the Muffinmobile, it's so strongly built. It will be as good as new even in a hundred years, when your grandchildren's children want to go on a tour!'

Vega didn't think the Muffinmobile looked especially well built. It looked as if it might fall apart if you poked it. A thick layer of dust covered it and a lot of spiders had built beautiful webs in the windows. Vega supposed that they all had transparent blood and were bad at keeping secrets.

'Now let me see, I should have some vegetable oil here somewhere...' Hector rolled his trolley over to the shelves behind the Muffinmobile. 'Here! Prima frying oil, straight from the burger kiosk down by the roundabout!'

Hector opened the can and poured some of the oil through a spigot into a big tank made of bent and welded baking trays. He opened the door to the driving seat and settled behind the steering wheel.

'Now let's see, where do I have the key... That's it!' He reached over to the little trolley and took out a matchbox that rattled. 'Here it is! The visibility pills can be a help too, so you don't disappear in the middle of everything.'

There was a little box with several compartments in the trolley. Each compartment had a pill in it. Hector opened the box and counted.

'Goodness, was it Tuesday yesterday? Then I was probably invisible, because I forgot to take my pill. Oh well, I had no visitors so maybe it was just as well. I'll want a hat, too!'

Hector took his round bowler hat from the trolley and put it on his head. Then he opened the matchbox, took out the key, put it in the ignition and turned it.

At first nothing happened. Vega and Nelson waited. Then they heard a sound like someone beating cake batter under the hood. Then a sizzling, as if someone were frying pancakes. The Muffinmobile coughed a few times to get rid of all the dust that had built up between the gears and the rollers. Then the car began to shake, and with a sound like violently fermenting dough, the engine started.

'Right, all ready for departure?' called Hector.

Vega, Nelson and Flor could hardly believe it. The Muffinmobile worked! The smell of freshly baked croissants wafted through the Paraphernalium. Flor barked in expectation and rushed around the car, sniffing hard.

'It smells great!' cried Nelson.

'Yes, that's the best thing about the Muffinmobile,' said

Hector, 'it's really one big baking machine! Every kilometre generates another tray of fresh muffins in the boot. It rolls like a bun, as we said. Come on, everyone, jump aboard!'

They drove out of the Paraphernalium, through the garden and out onto the road, down the mountain, towards town. Hector was happy to be showing off his Muffinmobile again; he happily honked and waved at passersby and offered them muffins. And true enough, the people they passed were very surprised. They stopped in their tracks, mouths and eyes wide open. They pointed and called out, took pictures and cheered. A Muffinmobile does not go unnoticed. Especially if the passengers are an old grandfather, two children and a gigantic dog.

# 12

# The giraffe has high blood pressure

THE MUFFINMOBILE had driven almost all the way through town when sirens started up behind them.

'Oh no!' Vega cried. 'We're being followed! It must be Dad and Viola again!'

'Hold on now, ragamuffins!' Hector suddenly swung off the main street and into a small alley.

'But Hector, this is the wrong way!' said Vega. 'We have to go straight ahead to the harbour. The ferry leaves for the Mainland in an hour!'

'I know another way,' said Hector with a grin. 'We'll confuse them a little.'

They drove out of the alley and into another street, turned left, right and left again.

'Trust me, small figment of my imagination. Have I ever let you down?'

Vega thought of the poster in the Paraphernalium, where Hector stood in his green coat and top hat, presenting Circus Hectoramus. No, Hector had never let her down. She wondered if she should tell him where they were going. It seemed wrong that he didn't know. But they were in too much of a hurry to explain.

'Vega!' Nelson called. He'd been sitting up on the roof and had called down through a pipe Hector had mounted between the roof and the chassis for carrying words or food. He called his invention a *snack-tube*.

'What is it, bluenose?' Hector called back through the pipe.

'We're heading out of town! Towards Narrowneck! We can't drive there, can we?'

'Narrowneck?' Vega froze.

No, not many would choose to drive down Narrowneck. As I said, only hunters, tourists and idiots ventured all the way down the narrow isthmus to the Torso. And to be honest, not many tourists came to Giraffe Island. And there weren't many hunters either.

'Hold your judgement,' said Hector. 'This is just a short-cut, see, to shake them off. No one will follow us here. Only idiots drive down the Neck.'

They drove past the Capital City's last houses, the last gardens of the houses, the last trees of the gardens, and the last branches of the last trees. When the sound of the sirens had died away, the road narrowed to a little gravel track and the sea opened out on both sides. The Muffinmobile jolted onto the peninsula. Water in all directions, as far as the eye could see. No trees, just rocks. Red granite against blue sea. The red rocks were the patches on the giraffe's neck. To the east, somewhere out of sight, lay the Mainland.

Flor stretched out through the car window and tasted the salt air on her tongue. One paw kept a firm hold on Nelson's leg up on the roof.

'Oh!' both children sighed. 'It's so beautiful!'

'Isn't it?' said Hector. 'It's good to be an idiot sometimes. The Narrowneck road is windy, dangerous and long, but it leads to the most beautiful place in the world.'

'To Giraffe's Heart?' asked Vega.

'Yes,' said Hector. 'To the Heart.'


THEY DROVE AND DROVE along Narrowneck. The wind bunted the Muffinmobile to and fro. The waffle-iron wheels only just fit on the narrow road. The smell of freshly baked muffins swirled across the water, and the seals and seahorses turned aerial somersaults, trying to catch a whiff.

A giraffe's neck is long, so long that you can't understand how it manages to be so long and still end in a complete head with a brain and eyes and everything a head should have. Or a town for that matter.

'Do giraffes often faint?' asked Vega. 'They have such long necks; they must walk round feeling dizzy and faint all the time.'

'They do! They faint all the time!' cried Nelson down the snack-tube. 'You only have to give them a poke and over they go PAFF PAFF PAFF—'

'No, they don't.' Hector capped the end of the pipe so that Nelson's voice disappeared. 'The giraffe actually has the highest blood pressure of all animals, and an unusually large heart that can pump blood all the way up the long neck. The giraffe's heart weighs twelve kilos, can you imagine? So, giraffes never get dizzy or faint, because the blood rushes up their neck at approximately one million kilometres an hour. They have such high blood pressure that they can't eat liquorice. I can't either according to the agents, but I take no notice.'

An unusually large heart, Vega thought. A bit like Dad. 'Will we be at the Heart soon?' she asked.

'Yes, soon. But we have to leave Narrowneck first, and drive onto the Torso. Then it's not far to Giraffe's Heart. It's the most beautiful lake you can imagine. In fact, one of the most beautiful in the whole world.'

'Have you seen the whole world, Hector?'

'As good as! And you can take my word for it, there's no place like the heart of this island. And no water as clear and sweet.'

*Pling!*

'Oh, there goes another tray of muffins. Flor, will you look after it?'

A few muffins later they had reached the other end of Narrowneck. The road widened, and the Muffinmobile drove out onto the wide-open Torso. Firs and pine trees and red cliffs as far as Vega could see. Ants waved and moose came up to say hello. Nelson fed them muffins. Forest, so much forest. It wasn't hard to imagine a humplefoot stamping around here among the trees, big and bellowing. What if they saw one?

THE ROAD GREW INDISTINCT, branching off in many directions, with fir trees and bushes grown up in the middle of it and rocks and stones scattered here and there. But Hector seemed to know exactly where to drive.

'Have you been to Giraffe's Heart many times, Hector?' Vega asked.

'Many, many times,' said Hector. 'But a long time ago. I used to come and collect sugar water from the Heart to water the garden with. These days the agents bring me lemonade from the shop. The plants don't get quite the oomph when you water with lemonade, but it's better than nothing.'

A streak of silver glinted somewhere on the horizon. The closer they came, the bigger the streak. It shimmered like diamonds in the autumn sun. When the Muffinmobile

drove up a hill the silver strip disappeared for a moment, then as they crested the top, there it was, bigger and shinier and more beautiful than anything Vega had ever seen.

'What a huge puddle!' Nelson shouted.

'I told you it was unusually large in relation to the body,' said Hector. 'That, my figments, is Giraffe's Heart. The absolute centre of Giraffe Island. This is the source of all love. And sugar water, of course.'

Giraffe's Heart was surrounded by forest and rocks. They drove along the lake till they came to a little beach. The Muffinmobile stopped with a hiss, like when you put your finger in yeasty dough. They got out of the car. It was still and silent. Hector walked in slow steps to the water's edge. Vega remembered the trolley he'd left at home in the Paraphernalium. It might be hard for him to walk without it. Hector crouched, cupped his hands, and dipped them into the water. He lifted his hands to his mouth and drank. Then he took another mouthful. And another. He drank and drank, as if he'd been thirsty for years.

Flor also went to the water's edge and began filling the bottles and thermoses she'd brought in her backpack. Vega and Nelson took off their shoes and socks, dipped first one toe each in the water, then both feet. Giraffe's Heart was warmer than Vega had expected. The autumn had frost on its breath, and the sea around Giraffe Island had long been too cold for swimming. But the water in Giraffe's Heart was warm and clear, like a big glass of lukewarm water. The surface was mirror-smooth, quite unaffected by the windy day.

Nelson waded out quickly and went right in, overalls and all. Vega took a few steps into the water. It quickly grew deep. She thought of what Hector often said, that no one had ever found the bottom of Giraffe's Heart. It might be deeper than the sea. How deep could a heart be? If it was terribly deep, how could you be sure there wasn't a monster in it? Something lurking below, that could attack at any moment? Like Dad's heart, which all at once had an elephant in it.

A sudden noise cut through the silence. Like the wailing they'd heard in Hector's garden. Vega froze. They'd seen nobody since they drove out of town onto Narrowneck.

'Hector?' she said. 'Don't you always say that only hunters, tourists and idiots come all the way out to the Torso?'

'So I do,' said Hector, still drinking.

'But do they sound like sirens?'

'No, only police cars sound like sirens. And fire engines. And wailing horns.'

The wailing drew closer, and at the far end of Giraffe's Heart, two cars appeared, driving so fast that the fir-babies and rock-puppies scuttled off in all directions. One car was Dad's. The other was large and white, like the sort of car that Hector's agents usually drove. That was the one wailing.

Hector stopped drinking and looked up.

'In the name of all one-legged greybeards! They must have followed the crumbs from the Muffinmobile! Quick, everyone!'

Vega, Flor and Hector hurried back to the car. Hector was much faster now, lighter, more agile. His back was straight, and he looked strong. Was it just because he was in a hurry and he'd forgotten he was old, or was it to do with the water from Giraffe's Heart?

'Come on, Nelson! Hurry!' Vega shouted.

Nelson, who was some way out, lying on his back and gurgling water, had to quickly swim ashore. The cars came closer. The siren howl swept over the mirror-calm lake and the water shuddered uneasily. Nelson rushed out of the water and over to the Muffinmobile. He threw himself into the back seat just as the cars reached the shore on the other side. Flor scooped up the children's socks and shoes and leaped in after Nelson.

'Now we're hooting!' cried Hector, planting his foot.

The Muffinmobile's engine sounded like someone popping popcorn and frying doughnuts, both at once. They reached such a speed that Vega couldn't see the road ahead anymore. The Muffinmobile zigzagged between fir trees and rocks, along the cliff edge with the water of

Giraffe's Heart gaping on one side and irritated moose on the other. Nelson shrieked and laughed as if he were on a roller coaster, while Flor sat still and hung onto him with her paws. Vega looked back. The cars were only a few metres behind them. She could see her father's rooftop eyebrows through the window, and Viola beside him, caught up in a whirling snowstorm.

'Hurry, Hector!' Vega cried. 'They'll catch us up!'

'No, they won't,' said Hector. 'This is not the first time the Muffinmobile and I have been on the run from idiots.'

Vega looked out towards Giraffe's Heart. The water had begun to swell and churn, as if agitated. Big waves washed in along the beach, splashing the Muffinmobile and the other cars.

Soon they'd left Giraffe's Heart behind. The forest thinned and the great plain of Torso appeared in front of them. The Muffinmobile drove faster and faster. Her father and the agents followed.

'Hector!' Vega shrieked. 'There's no escape! We can't go this way! There's no harbour! The island is running out!'

'Trust me, small figment of my imagination,' Hector said calmly, and he sped on over the rugged plain. Now they could see the sea. The vast, wild sea, the deep blue of a giraffe's tongue. It drew closer and closer, and Hector drove straight at it.

'No, Hector! Turn around!'

'Trust me, I said.'

The rocky cliffs were approaching at breakneck speed. The children screamed. Flor barked. Hector put his foot down.

And here was the cliff edge. Vega didn't dare look. She felt it: flying free through the air for seconds on end. She took a deep breath and squeezed her eyes tight; mermaids and dolphins were swirling behind her lids, and SMACK they hit the water and . . . they didn't sink. Vega opened her eyes. The Muffinmobile was afloat!

Hector pushed a button on the dashboard, and from the sides of the Muffinmobile propellors made from old baking trays appeared and began to spin. The Muffinmobile glided slowly over the water with a quiet whisking sound.

'Did you really think I'd build a car that couldn't go on water?' Hector asked, laughing.

'Giddy guinea pigs!' Nelson gasped. 'That's the most exciting thing I've ever done! I thought we were about to drown like land-loving gerbils! Can we do it again?'

Vega looked back. The cars had stopped at the cliff edge, and Dad and Viola had got out. Viola's eyes shone and her hair whirled in the blizzard surrounding her. A film of ice spread slowly over the water below the cliff. And even though Viola and Dad became smaller and smaller the further the Muffinmobile drove out to sea, Vega could clearly see her father's heart through his jacket, big and blue and coated in ice.

# A shrimp's heart is in its head

DAY WAS TURNING into evening. The sun had coloured the sky above the horizon pink and orange, but the water was as blue as before. The Muffinmobile had been going for a couple of hours, past the small islands and skerries off the east coast of Giraffe Island, and was now chugging along in open water. They couldn't see land in any direction. Flor had taken out the sandwiches and poured hot chocolate. She shared the muffins fairly between them. At sea, the Muffinmobile didn't bake as many muffins as on land, so they had to make do with a couple every nautical mile.

Nelson sat on the roof, rattling off facts about various sea creatures from his notebook. Vega climbed up and sat beside him. A little seahorse was doing somersaults and tricks in the water alongside the Muffinmobile. It whinnied and winked at Vega. She wondered if she could ride a seahorse underwater, if it ate seagrass instead of real grass, and if it liked being patted on the nose. She took out her sketchpad and drew the seahorse, with hooves and a tail and a long billowing mane of seaweed.

'Hey, we're on our way,' Nelson said softly, nudging Vega in the side with his elbow. 'Soon we'll reach Kingstown, and the circus. Think how many fantastic things we'll have to document there! Not to mention that we might find your mother, Katja, and the answer to the Circature Mystery.'

Nelson had decided it took too long to say the ice-water-fire-circus mystery, so he'd begun calling it the Circature Mystery, a blend of circus and temperature. He'd called it the Temperacus Mystery for a while but didn't think it had the right ring to it.

'Mm,' said Vega. The thought of Katja being her mother still didn't feel right. Like a jumper that was a little too tight. 'But what if Dad and Viola keep following us?' she said. 'They might jump on the ferry and get to Kingstown before we do.'

'Oh, they don't know where we're going. Even if they got back to Capital City before the ferry left, they won't be there till tomorrow. Those floating cities go much slower than the Muffinmobile. We'll make it to the circus before they catch up.'

Vega tried to feel reassured by Nelson's words, but she couldn't stop thinking about Dad and his heart as he'd stood at the edge of the cliff looking after the Muffinmobile.

Was it really the right decision to leave him with Viola? Could she have kidnapped him, forced him to come along and find her mother? And there was Hector, whom they'd more or less forced to come, without telling him where they were going. Dad and Hector were the only people who'd ever looked after her, but now it felt as if she'd left them both. And here she was, bobbing over the sea, further and further from Giraffe Island. She'd never been so far from home.

'I wonder if we should tell Hector we're on our way to the circus,' she said.

'No,' Nelson said, 'not now. We can't risk him getting upset and turning around.'

'But it feels bad lying to him.'

'We're not lying! We're just not telling everything. The logic is simple. You think too much with your feelings! You're like a shrimp! Did you know that shrimps have their heart in their head? They hardly know the difference between thinking and feeling, just like you.'

The sun sent its last rays as a glittering farewell, and then lay down in the sea. The moon yawned, stretched and rose higher in the sky. Night fell. Hector put the Muffinmobile on autopilot to Kingstown and lay down on the back seat. The children huddled together on the roof, and Flor put a

127

blanket over them. Then she sat beside them and looked out over the sea. There was nothing to see but sea and night. But someone had to keep watch.

THE SCREECH OF SEAGULLS found its way into Vega's dream. The sound started as a honk. Then it became a shriek, so loud that it exploded and turned into a fire engine that drove faster and faster through a snowy landscape looking for a fire to put out. Vega opened her eyes slowly. The first thing she saw was Flor, looking at her mildly and wagging her tail.

'Good morning,' said Vega, sitting up.

The sun was already high in the sky. The sea rippled blue, so sparkly it dazzled her. She squinted. Directly ahead was a stretch of tall buildings and smoking chimneys. Kingstown! They'd arrived!

Vega helped Flor wake the others, and soon Hector sat wide awake at the wheel and Nelson on the roof squawking along with the seagulls.

'Ahoy! Left! Right! Starboard! Spin the wheel! Reef the sails! Hoist the box! Shake your belly!' Nelson called down through the snack-tube, and Hector tried his best to follow the instructions to navigate the Muffinmobile into the harbour.

They drew in at the ferry dock, where the harbour folk stood in their reflective vests and woolly hats, fat ropes at the ready to hold the floating cities in check. The Muffinmobile chugged up to the ramp, retracted its propellors and continued ashore on all four wheels. The harbour people's jaws dropped. Hector waved cheerfully and Vega and Nelson tossed them muffins as they drove by.

'So there, ragamuffins,' said Hector. 'Here we are in Kingstown! What do you want to do here? Go to the amusement park? Buy toys? Pick berries?'

'We're going to Keytree Park,' said Nelson, with a wink at Vega. 'We heard it's very nice.'

'Keytree Park!' said Hector. 'I've been there many times. Very nice. Almost the only key trees in the world grow there. I took cuttings for my own key trees from there once upon a time. They've grown very well. Vega, you've seen what beautiful heavy keys they bear in the summer. They're very good towards autumn when they get a little rusty. Excellent with cream and prune puree.'

The Muffinmobile carried on through Kingstown. Vega, who'd never been in a town other than Capital City on Giraffe Island, couldn't believe her eyes. The buildings were tall and grey and looked bored and snobbish, as if all they had to do was try to outgrow the other houses. The streets were wide and full of cars that tooted and glared at one another. There were cafes and shops on every corner, and people went in and out of them without looking at each other. They wore smart clothes and stared at little glowing rectangles in their hands or talked loudly into thin air.

Maybe all the residents of Kingstown had their own imaginary animals that only they could see?

The town was so big it felt like it would never end. The buildings passed by in big grid patterns that reminded Vega of her maths book. In the middle of the grid, there was suddenly a gap, like an empty field where you could draw or write whatever you wanted. The gap was green and filled with leafy trees that bristled with keys.

'There you are! This is Keytree Park!' Hector said triumphantly. 'Kingstown's oasis, as they call it. Legend has it that the first king of the country dropped the castle key somewhere in the garden. He searched and searched but couldn't find it. He dug up everybody's gardens looking for the key, but at last he gave up and stormed his own castle to get inside. In time, small key trees began to grow, and this park came into being. The castle fell down and became compost for all the trees. The king died.'

Vega giggled at her grandfather's story. She'd learned at school that Keytree Park in Kingstown had got its name from someone called Nikodemus Keybaum, but she preferred Hector's explanation.

The Muffinmobile drove into the park. The road was straight and edged with rocks and flowerbeds arranged in geometric patterns. It was a bit like driving around Hector's garden, except here someone had arranged everything into knife-sharp mathematical shapes. Large, stately key trees flanked the straight road. They drove past a statue of a dragon spouting a shower of flowers from its nostrils, while small stone cherubs flew around trying to catch the flowers in their baskets. Some marble lions stood guarding a flight of steps that led to a pavilion. They were much better kept than the stone lions at Lotsberget at home on Giraffe Island. But they still waved at Vega as the Muffinmobile drove by.

A little further on was a field where something big and red loomed above the treetops. A tent.

Something began to move in Vega's backpack; it quivered and jumped as if a whole swarm of flying hamsters were inside it.

Janna's letter had woken up.

'Well, what do you want to do here then?' asked Hector. 'Pick keys? Do somersaults? Fish for goldfish in the pond?'

'We'll... we're...' Vega looked at Nelson and he nodded. 'We're going to the circus. In the tent over there is a circus called Circus Rumbunctus. I have a friend there we're going to visit. It's my pen pal, Janna, who I told you about.'

At that moment the Muffinmobile coughed and came to a standstill. Smoke poured from the engine, which gave off a smell of burning.

'I think the muffins have burnt,' Hector said quietly. 'I'll need to have a look at the engine.'

He climbed slowly from the car and rolled up the sleeves of his old jersey. The little giraffe on his arm looked at Vega and smiled sadly. Vega instinctively put her hand to her own arm. Nelson dug Vega in the side.

'We have to go to the circus!' Nelson whispered. 'We're so close now. We have to find Janna and talk to her before the show. And before your father and Code V catch up with us.'

'But we can't leave him here.' Vega hesitated as they stepped out of the car.

'Hector, we have to go to the circus now,' she said. 'It's important.'

'Off you go,' said Hector, his head under the bonnet. 'I'll stay here and fix the Muffinmobile.'

'Hector, please come with us.'

'I'm saying no.' Hector's voice was wet with rain. Vega had never heard him sound like that. 'I don't like the circus. I'm staying here.'

'Come on, Vega, we're going without him,' said Nelson. 'Flor can carry us the last bit.'

Vega turned and climbed onto Flor's back. 'Hector?'

'What is it?' Her grandfather's voice came from under the hood. Only his curly hair stuck out. The hat fell off.

Vega sighed. 'Thanks for the ride.'

# Every zebra has
# a different pattern

VEGA SAT STIFF, solemn and silent on the dog's back, steering firmly towards the circus tent. Nelson was excited as usual. He also talked non-stop as usual, probably more from nervousness than from having much to say.

When they came closer to the tent, they saw various animals grazing. There was a herd of zebras with different patterns. Some elephants with rumpled trunks. They reminded Vega of her little wardrobe mammoth. And there were tigers with long sharp front teeth, ostriches with funny hats, lions with coloured manes. So many animals. Nelson rubbed his eyes.

'Did you know that the tiger is the world's biggest cat? That the lion is the only feline with a mane? Did you know that no zebra pattern is the same as any other? That elephants eat a hundred and fifty kilos of food a day?' He burbled on, clutching the ruff of Flor's neck with one

hand and trying to pull out *Nelson's Interesting Facts* with the other. 'Look, there's a zebra with zigzag stripes! And a camel with three humps! The programme was right, they sure do have unusual animals here!'

Flor carried on towards the tent. It was striped red and yellow, held up by thick ropes staked to the ground. Colourful bunting and lanterns hung in the trees all around. They could hear music and laughter.

The closer they got, the more Vega was filled with an unfamiliar feeling, like a warm wave. It simmered and seethed like a stew; it smelled new and different, wild, foreign, colourful. Her backpack jumped and glowed; the letter inside had gone mad, the flying hamsters had grown into pig-bats that longed to come out and flap around among all the people and gossip about the dangers they'd met on their travels.

Here they were at last. This was where they'd get their answers. Nelson asked the question foremost in Vega's mind.

'How shall we find Janna?'

Vega had no idea what Janna looked like. She gazed around. The area outside the tent was full of people. Acrobats were stretching in their glittery sequin suits, a man was balancing a sword on his tongue, a gang of clowns were busy stuffing their bellies with cushions and a fortune-teller was polishing her crystal ball. Everywhere things glimmered and rattled and sparkled and tinkled.

It was as if they'd gone through the little closet in Hector's Paraphernalium and into a new world. Maybe that closet turned into this world when it rained in Hector's garden and everything in the house swelled up? Vega promised herself she'd go and look next time she visited the house on a rainy day. Her heart clenched at the thought of her grandfather. But now wasn't the time to worry.

People were talking and laughing, and no one took any notice of Flor and the children. Vega had never felt so normal. She suddenly realised that her mother might be here somewhere in all the confusion. The circus director, perhaps. Katja.

'Was there anything in Janna's letter about where she usually is or what she does?' asked Nelson. 'Otherwise it's like looking for hay in a needle factory.'

'No, I don't think so...' Vega went through the letter in her head. She'd read it so many times she almost knew it by heart. 'I know!' she cried. 'The ponies! She said she feeds four-leaf clovers to the ponies before the show!'

The children and Flor ran back through the crowds to where all the animals were grazing. There was a small herd of pink ponies beside a collection of rose bushes. The little ponies whinnied when they saw Flor. She was bigger than any of them.

'Imagine, they've painted their ponies pink!' said Nelson. 'Or they might have given them rhinoceros milk to drink. What a place!'

There was a girl crouched amongst the roses, feeding the ponies grass. She spoke quietly to them and stroked their muzzles.

Nelson went over to the girl and leaned nonchalantly against one of the rose bushes.

'Do the horses like the grass here?' he asked, reaching for a fistful of grass which he stuffed into his mouth. He chewed thoughtfully without taking his eyes off the girl.

The girl looked up and smiled a little. She had blonde feathery hair and light grey eyes. Her thin lips looked as if they wanted to smile all the time, and her teeth looked as if they were protesting because they were ashamed of their many gaps.

'Yes, it's fine. They like four-leaf clovers even better, but I couldn't find enough today for all of them.'

'I actually have a tube of honey with me,' said Nelson. 'Maybe we could stick an extra leaf on the three-leaf clovers?'

'What a good idea!'

'Are you Janna?' Vega asked shyly.

The girl stood up. 'Yes, that's me. Who are you?'

'I'm Vega. Your pen pal.'

Janna's thin lips stretched into an enormous smile. 'Vega! I didn't think you'd come!' Janna threw her arms around Vega. Vega had never been hugged by another child. It felt a little strange. 'I'm so happy to meet you!'

Janna let Vega go and looked at her closely. Janna's light

grey eyes and fair curls, and Vega's dark brown eyes and black corkscrew curls.

'You're like two zebras!' Nelson said. 'Almost the same, but different if you look carefully. It really is true that no zebra has exactly the same stripes as another!'

Nelson opened his notebook and wrote *Vega* and *Janna* on the page about zebra facts so he'd remember the example. Then he did a little pirouette and bowed his head all the way to the ground.

'And my name is Nelson,' he said.

'Nice to meet you,' said Janna.

'Likewise. And this is Flor.'

Flor ambled over and nuzzled Janna's hand.

'Wow!' Janna said. 'From the corner of my eye I thought she was one of the ponies!'

'Yes, it's possible she's half horse,' said Nelson. 'Her family tree is not very clear. But we haven't come here to talk about ponies and zebras all day! We have an urgent mission — isn't that right, Vega?'

Vega nodded.

'Janna,' she said, 'you have to help us with something. It's a bit complicated. I haven't had time to explain it all in a letter, everything's happened so fast. But... we think my mother might be somewhere here at the circus. And maybe you know her.'

JANNA TOOK VEGA, Nelson and Flor to the back of the tent where the circus people had their wagons. They were set up like a miniature town, with a big patch of grass in the middle. Each wagon was painted in its own design, with a big letter on it. Nelson spelt out the letters.

'T...R...U...N...C...U...S  C...R...U...M...B...U...S...C...I What? Who's Truncus Crumbusci? Is that one of the artists?'

'It says Circus Rumbunctus!' Janna giggled. 'The wagons are just out of order. Sometimes it says Curium Bunccrusts or something else silly.'

Janna went over to the wagon with an M on it. It was green with red stars in different sizes.

'This is where I live!' she said. 'I don't think anyone's home just now. Katja is putting on her make-up in the costume wagon and Phoenix is preparing the animals for the opening act.'

Janna opened the door and signalled the others to come in. Flor lay outside the door and kept watch.

Janna made a sweeping gesture around the little space.

'Well, this is the hall, the sitting room, the kitchen, the bedroom, the office and the dining room. And that's the whole tour done.' Janna smiled.

Vega thought of her apartment at home in Capital City. Her own room, where she could be alone, do her homework and draw and anything else she wanted, and still have room for mammoths and polar bears. How would any of her animals find room in this wagon? Even Flor had to wait outside.

'Cool!' said Nelson, and he went around the caravan inspecting everything. 'A foldaway sink, a dining table that opens into a bed, a bath that can be a toilet... Wouldn't this be something for your grandfather, Vega? I mean, he built the Muffinmobile, so he'd find all of this really interesting.'

Vega's heart nipped again at the thought of Hector.

'The mystery!' she cried. 'Nelson, get out your notebook and explain everything to Janna!'

Nelson took out *Nelson's Mysteries and Such* and carefully looked up the pages with *Circature Mystery*. He sat down at the table in the dining room/bedroom/sitting room, and Janna sat across from him. Then he explained everything to her in detail. He told about Vega's dad and the ice queen Viola, about the ice and the snow in the apartment, and how they'd looked for a way to rescue Vega's dad from Viola and the chill and realised that her mother, always described as fiery and warm, was the only antidote. He told about finding the old circus poster in Hector's garage, and how it had coincided so strangely with Vega suddenly becoming pen pals with Janna, who lived at a circus, and how through the equation $x + 24v - 0° + y = 100\%$ they'd realised that Vega's mother must live at the circus — and that, by the way, they were pretty sure it was Janna's mother, Katja. He also told how they'd fled from Giraffe Island in Hector's Muffinmobile, that they'd been chased by Vega's father and

Viola, who, by the way, were likely still on their trail and could turn up at any moment. He said all this in practically a single breath. Then he fell silent and looked expectantly at Janna.

'Do you understand?'

'I think so,' Janna said, looking at Vega. 'So, you think you're going to find your mother here at the circus?'

Vega nodded.

'And then you think she'll go back with you to Giraffe Island to help your father escape from another woman?'

Vega nodded.

'And you think that my mother, Katja, could be your mother?'

Vega nodded.

Janna was quiet for a moment, then she looked at Nelson. 'What makes you think that?'

'The Circature Mystery, the equation, the programme, the Hectoramus and Rumbuc — how could it be clearer?' Nelson sounded as if he was trying to explain 2 + 2 to a sloth.

Janna giggled.

'Sorry, but Katja doesn't look a bit like you, Vega. Besides, she's actually blonde — she's just dyed her hair red. And she's very tall and quite fat. And she's loud and noisy. I'm sorry, but I don't think Katja is your mother.'

Vega didn't think so either. And she and Janna looked so different, even if Nelson thought they were as alike as two zebras. They could never have had the same mother. Janna was somehow light, like a feather or a little warm breeze. Vega had never felt like a wind.

The paper doll in Vega's head washed off its green eyeshadow. A small bumblesnozz buzzed at the window, bumping into the glass. Vega caught it in her hands, stroked its furry back and released it out the door.

'Okay,' said Nelson. 'The equation has changed; I'll have to recalculate. But it's still possible that Vega's mother is here somewhere.

'She could still be at this circus, don't you think, Vega?'

Vega said nothing, but Janna replied.

'Absolutely! From what I can see of this mystery, anything's possible.'

Janna let her gaze wander over the page about the Circature Mystery.

'So, you don't know your mother's name?' she asked.

Nelson and Vega looked at each other. Both shook their heads.

'Or what she looks like?' asked Janna.

Vega and Nelson looked at each other again. They hadn't managed to take the portrait of Vega's mother from Hector. Vega had looked at it a million times and she knew exactly what it looked like, but right now she could remember only one thing.

'She's got dark curly hair. Like me. Or had, anyway.'

'And she's supposed to be fiery!' said Nelson. 'Or warm in some way. We think.'

Janna had a cunning look. 'Then I have a suggestion! Or wait. Maybe not quite...'

'Let's hear it!' Nelson had opened a new page in his notebook and sat, pen poised.

'Well, it *could* be a person called Olga. She's a fire-eater and she juggles burning torches and things. She has long dark hair, but it's not curly.'

'It must be her!' Nelson cried. 'A fire-eater! That sounds tough!'

Olga. The paper doll tested the name. It pulled its curly hair out until it was long and straight and snorted a small flame from one nostril. The paper doll had puffed out fire like a dragon long before Vega knew anything about the circus. Her mother, fire-eater Olga. It was true.

'We can go and ask her right now,' Janna said. 'She usually warms up behind the tent before a show. Haha. Warms up. Get it?'

Janna started laughing. Nelson quickly took out his tape recorder and spoke into it quietly:

'Laugh number thirty-three.' He held the tape recorder in front of Janna. Her laugh was bright and whinnying, just like one of the small ponies.

'Five seconds,' said Nelson when he'd turned off the tape recorder. 'Perfect.'

# 15

# A dragonfly lives for a year as a nymph, one hour as an adult

IT WAS AN UNREAL FEELING. In just a few minutes Vega might meet her mother and have answers to everything. What would she say? Would her mother even be happy to see her?

Janna led them back through the little town of circus wagons at the back of the tent. They passed the group of clowns. They all had big bellies and red noses. One of them held a flower out to Nelson.

'Oh thanks!' he cried and, the moment he reached for the flower, water sprayed in his face.

He burst out laughing. 'What a great trick,' he snorted, 'a flower that sprays water, did you see? This is the most fun place I've ever been to! I wish I could move here and be a clown! Or a lion tamer! Or a juggler! Or a tightrope walker! Or a sword-eater! Or—'

'There she is,' Janna said.

A few metres in front of them stood the fire-eater, Olga. Vega couldn't take her eyes from her. She was beautiful, with long brown hair and a skirt of rattling chains. 'Come on, let's go and talk to her!' said Nelson.

'But what shall we say?' asked Vega. 'What if it's her?'

'We have to think of something only your mother would know. For example, if she recognises your birthmark. If she's your mother, she should remember that.'

Vega had been so busy trying to think how she would recognise her mother, it hadn't occurred to her that there might be something her mother would recognise about her. She suddenly remembered Hector saying once that their giraffe birthmark ran in the family.

'My grandfather has one like this. Maybe my mother has too.'

'Does your grandfather have that same birthmark?' cried Nelson. 'Why didn't you say? That changes everything. It turns the whole equation upside down!'

'Why's that?'

'I don't know, but I'd better write it down anyway in *Nelson's Mysteries and Such*. Come on, we have to go over to her and have a look!'

Janna went and lay down with Flor, who sensed it was best to stay in the background.

Olga the fire-eater was talking to a man with enormous ears that lay folded double on his shoulders. Vega and Nelson crept over to them. Olga had a green shawl over her shoulders, and under it a beaded corset. Her arms were bare but hidden by the shawl. There was no sign of a birthmark. Nelson took out his magnifying glass and crept closer. They were right beside her before she noticed them.

'Gosh!' She looked at the children with a small laugh. 'What's going on here? Who are you?'

'My name is ... Simeon Somersault,' said Nelson, bowing deeply. 'I've come to the circus to do a little investigation.'

'Well, that's exciting,' said Olga.

Vega couldn't say a word.

'Yes, and this is my companion ... Dana Daydream,' Nelson went on.

'Nice to meet you, Dana,' said Olga, smiling at Vega.

The smile hit Vega right in the stomach. She staggered a little.

'Well, we wanted to ask you a few questions,' said Nelson.

'Sure, fire away,' said Olga.

Nelson cleared his throat. 'Firstly, we're wondering how long you've been at the circus.'

'Not very long,' said Olga. 'I came here with my father a few years ago.'

Nelson gave Vega a look. 'Your father, did you say? Tell us a little more about him.'

'Well, I don't really know what he's up to these days. But he was also a circus artist. One of the best. He taught me all I know. He was a fantastic acrobat, expert at juggling and building things.'

Nelson looked at Vega again.

'But he's no longer here at the circus,' Olga continued. 'He got very angry and quit when we got a new circus director.'

'Aha,' said Nelson. 'Why did the old circus director quit?'

'I'm not quite sure what happened,' said Olga. 'I think it was an accident of some kind. Some say he sabotaged an act, but I don't believe that. He disappeared very suddenly.'

'Interesting,' said Nelson. 'Very interesting. We have just one more question, then we'll leave you alone.'

'No problem.'

Olga's eyes were sharp, her pupils ringed in shimmering gold. To Vega they looked like rings of fire. She felt a wave of heat come over her, as if she were sitting in a sauna. How could Olga feel so hot, but not really be warm? What would happen to Dad's frozen heart if he faced such ferocious fire?

'Would you mind showing us if you have a birthmark on your arm?' Nelson continued boldly. 'I realise it's a bit forward, but it's for a very important collection of statistics on the different types of marks found on circus performers.'

Olga laughed and took off her shawl. Her arms looked

strong, and the left one had a
tattoo of a dragon. The right
arm had nothing.

'Nice dragon!' said Nelson.
'Fire-breathing, just like you. I get
the joke. You don't happen to have
any interesting facts about dragons?'

Vega tugged at Nelson's arm.
He cleared his throat.

'Thank you from both of us. You'll
receive information about our investigation
by post. Everything is of course confidential. Bye-bye, apple
pie!'

Nelson began walking back to Janna and Flor. Vega
turned and looked at Olga. The fire-eater smiled and waved.

A dragon. But no giraffe.

'So, we can delete that possibility,' Nelson said. 'I thought
so as soon as she said her father was a fantastic acrobat.
Your grandfather is the stiffest old man I've ever seen.'

'Yes, I guess,' said Vega. 'But wasn't it strange what she
said about the circus director? That he just disappeared,
maybe because of an accident?'

'Super strange,' said Nelson. 'I think we should ask the
next suspect more about it.'

'The next?'

'Well, we have to keep looking! We can't just give up.
This is it, right now! You've been waiting for this all your

life! You're like a dragonfly who's lived their whole life as a nymph and now has the chance to be a dragonfly. But only for a single day, because then you die. Some dragonflies live a whole year as a nymph, then only a single hour as a dragonfly — did you know that? They have almost no chance to be themselves. So it's time to stop being a nymph. Get it?'

Vega nodded. Imagine what it was like to be a dragonfly. Knowing you had only one hour to do everything you'd dreamed of while you were a little creeping nymph. See the world, slide down a rainbow, find friends and drink dew from flower petals. Imagine knowing you might not have time for all that.

'That's why we have to keep looking,' said Nelson, as they went back to Flor and Janna. 'We're getting closer to the solution; I can feel it! Don't forget I'm half worm!'

Nelson sat down in the grass and accepted Flor's wet facewash.

'Janna,' he said, 'is there anyone else at the circus who could be Vega's mother? Fiery? Curly hair? Fiery curls? Curly fire?'

'Yes, I have thought of somebody,' said Janna. She twirled a three-leaf clover between her fingers. 'One of the clowns has dark curly hair. Cindy. She's really nice. She always goes around giving people hugs. And she's funny.' Cindy the clown. Nice and funny with curly hair.

The paper doll in Vega's head stopped blowing fire and

instead put on a red clown nose and a pair of big striped trousers. Then it started laughing and gave Vega a hug. Maybe her hugs were warm enough to melt the ice covering her dad's heart. My mother, Cindy the clown, Vega thought.

It could be.

 16

# Pigs can't sweat

'THAT'S HER with the green trousers and the really big shoes,' said Janna.

Nelson took Vega's hand and followed Janna before Vega had time to think. They pushed through the cheerful clowns who threw confetti at them and conjured coins from behind their ears, over to a clown who stood juggling colourful balls. She had a big belly, a red jacket, green pants, very long shoes, and dark curly hair in a messy bun.

'Cindy?' Janna said to the clown.

The clown looked at the children. She wasn't wearing a clown nose, but her face was painted white, and her big red mouth went all the way to her ears. It was quite hard to imagine what she looked like without make-up, but Vega thought she was very beautiful anyway. The paper doll painted its mouth big and red.

'Janna, my little owl!' cried Cindy, lifting Janna in a big hug.

'Why does she call her an owl?' Nelson whispered to Vega. 'From what I've seen Janna has neither three eyelids nor a head she can turn full circle.'

'Cindy,' said Janna, once Cindy had put her down, 'these are my friends, Nelson and—'

'Excuse me, Mrs Clown,' Nelson interrupted, shushing Janna. 'My name is . . . Malte af Goldhair. And this is my companion, Carmen Gooseberry.'

'Greetings, Malte and Carmen!' laughed the clown. 'My name's Cindy. How are you today?'

'Very well, thank you,' said Nelson. 'We're big admirers of clowns and the clown profession as a whole, and we hoped to ask you a few questions about what it's like to be a clown in today's circus environment.'

'Of course,' said Cindy, looking at Vega. She had light blue eyes that sparkled like sunlit sea. Vega felt dizzy and had to look away.

'Excellent,' said Nelson. 'I'd like to start by asking you how long you've been working as a clown?'

'It's been quite a few years now,' said Cindy. 'Before that I worked as an acrobat, but I had an accident so I can't do those tricks anymore.'

'Well,' said Nelson, 'may I ask what happened?'

'One of the lines broke. It was a perfectly ordinary performance, I was swinging from one trapeze to another with a few flips. When I grabbed the second trapeze, the rope broke, and I fell. I landed quite badly on my hip.'

'That sounds hard,' said Nelson. 'What happened then?'

'Well, after that, I couldn't do the necessary movements. I learned to juggle instead and started working as a clown. And it's actually much more fun! You don't have to risk your life every time, and you can make people happy.'

Cindy spoke quickly and easily, with laughter bubbling under the surface. Her body seemed full of energy. Her hands waved as she talked, and she almost seemed to be keeping herself from breaking into a dance. Vega didn't feel at all nervous, as she'd been with Olga the fire-eater. She could have carried on listening to her forever. She hoped the next question would give them the answer, that Cindy really was her mother.

'I used to sweat like a pig before I went up on stage, but now I just feel excited and happy before every show,' Cindy continued. 'Like now! It'll soon be time again!'

'Just a small interjection, Mrs Clown,' said Nelson, pointing a finger. 'Pigs are unable to sweat. It's in *Nelson's Interesting Facts*. And I, Malte af Goldhair, have read that book more times than a bee must visit a flower to make a dessertspoon of honey.'

Cindy laughed again.

'And how many times is that?'

'Four thousand.'

Vega saw bees flying around Cindy, gently humming their calm, monotonous song. They formed a circle around her, like a great buzzing sun. Cindy was wonderful.

155

'Oh, right. I'll take your word for it,' said Cindy. 'Let's say I was sweating like a horse. They sweat, right?'

'Oh yes!' said Nelson. 'And you can use their sweat as soap! I do that sometimes. Well, back to the investigation. If I may ask, did anything else happen after the accident? What did the circus director say about it, for example?'

Cindy took a long balloon from the pocket of her large pants and began twisting and tying it as she spoke. 'I don't know. I passed out right after my fall. I was in bed for several weeks after the accident. When I recovered, we had a new circus director, called Katja.'

'Oh, Katja!' said Nelson. 'What do you think of her?'

'Well, she's good. But she's not like . . . our last one. No one can replace him.'

The long balloon now had four legs and a body, and Cindy was almost finished with the head. Her hands worked quickly and automatically, her eyes fixed on Nelson and Vega.

'May I ask the name of the former circus director?' Nelson asked. 'You didn't happen to be related to him in some way?'

Vega's body tensed. The bees stopped buzzing.

Cindy was about to answer when one of the other clowns stepped forward in very large shoes and tapped her on the shoulder. 'Cindy, we have to get ready, the show's about to start. Where's your nose?'

Cindy laughed and fished a little red ball from the pocket of her big pants.

'I'm coming!' she said to the clown as she popped the ball onto her nose. 'Sorry guys, I have to go.'

Cindy handed the balloon animal to Vega.

'This one's for you, Carmen Gooseberry,' Cindy said quietly. The bees buzzed.

'Okay, but wait, one last thing!' said Nelson. 'Could we please look at your arms? We're also doing a study on... circus arms.'

Cindy took off her red jacket as she began walking slowly backwards towards the other clowns. She spun a little pirouette. Her arms were smooth and brown.

'Nice arms!' she laughed. 'Put that in your research! And no, I wasn't related to him. But he has a daughter!'

Cindy ran after the other clowns and disappeared into the mass of colours and big bellies.

'Not a pig or a horse, not an emu either, because they can't walk backwards,' said Nelson. 'And definitely not your mother.'

Vega looked down at the balloon animal in her hands. A giraffe.

# 17

# Snakes have
# no eyelids

VEGA AND NELSON stood looking after Cindy.

Nelson sighed. 'Oh. It would have been fun if she was your mother.'

'It would,' said Vega.

The paper doll pulled off its clown nose. It didn't even have curly hair now. It was just... bare.

Janna and Flor came over. Flor hugged Vega. 'So it wasn't her either?' asked Janna.

Vega and Nelson shook their heads.

'Then I'm sorry but I don't know who it could be,' said Janna.

'There must be another clue!' Nelson said. 'Something other than her being warm or having curly hair. Or having strange marks on her arms.'

'We don't know anything about her,' said Vega. 'I don't

know any more than that. I...I don't even know that.'

'But you know who you are!' said Nelson. 'She must be like you in some way! We can just look for something typical of you, and your mother should have at least some of the same thing. Don't you reckon?'

'Yes, but... There's nothing that's typical of me.'

'There is! Something you're especially good at? Something you love doing?'

'I don't know, I...'

Vega had never considered what was special about her. She tried to remember if she'd ever been given a compliment, but she couldn't think of one. She was probably just ordinary. Except for having no mother. But she had no talents, not like Olga who could breathe fire or Cindy who could juggle.

'Dad says I'm pretty good at jumping rope. I usually skip with the rubber monkeys in the schoolyard.'

'Jump-rope!' Nelson said. 'Is there anyone here at the circus who's good at skipping? Or doing anything with ropes? Any sort of jumping?'

Janna thought about it.

'Actually, there is a woman,' she said, 'a rope charmer. She used to charm snakes, but they escaped into the crowd. People didn't understand that they were harmless, so she had to stop with snakes and start with ropes instead. She's pretty weird. Well, I think so.' Janna leaned forward and whispered, 'I think she's a witch.'

Vega suddenly felt sick. Nelson's eyes were as wide as saucers.

'What's her name?' he whispered.

'Her name is... Ursula.'


THE AFTERNOON SUN shone low. It felt as if they'd been at the circus forever. The letters in Vega's backpack had stopped fluttering. The butterflies in her stomach too.

Soon the show would begin.

'We don't have much time,' said Janna.

The rope charmer's wagon was on the edge of the little circus town behind the tent. They passed all the other wagons. There were magicians shaking lost rabbits out of their hats, silent mimes polishing invisible cubes, and strong men and women doing push-ups. Vega saw the man with the big ears Olga the fire-eater had been talking to. He stood and flapped his ears, faster and faster, until his feet lifted a few centimetres from the ground. Everywhere, final preparations were being made for the day's performance.

They arrived at the rope charmer's wagon. The door was closed. 'She doesn't tend to come out much,' Janna said quietly. 'She just comes out to do her rope act, then returns to her wagon.'

The wagon was painted dark red with a pattern of black snakes winding around a large green S. There were a few chairs outside.

The buzz of the circus performers died away. All that remained was a silence that sounded like a single note.

They knocked on the door.

'I've never heard of anyone who can charm ropes,' Nelson whispered. 'Or snakes, for that matter. What if she looks like a snake? If she doesn't blink, she's a snake, because snakes don't have eyelids.'

Heavy footsteps sounded from inside the wagon. The door opened with a creak.

The woman standing in the doorway wore a long, dark-green dress and a pearl necklace. Her thick black hair rested in a braid on one shoulder. It was hard to tell how old she was. Her face was pale and had no wrinkles, but there were

white strands in the black braid. Her eyes were dark blue like the deepest night sky.

'Hello,' said Nelson. He took a deep breath to say more, but no words came out.

The woman looked at him for several seconds. Nelson held his breath. It looked like her eyes were trying to penetrate Nelson's head. He trembled a little.

'Hi,' she said at last, and the shadow of a smile played across her lips. Nelson breathed out.

'Who are you?'

'My name is... Nelson,' Nelson said. 'This is... Vega.'

'Nelson and Vega are my friends from Giraffe Island,' Janna explained. 'They just have a few questions for you.'

Janna leaned towards Nelson and Vega and said quietly, 'I have to go now.'

'No, please don't go!' Nelson hissed.

'I have to,' Janna whispered, 'the show starts any minute now, and I have to help Phoenix with the animals in the opening act. I hope you have time to go in! See you after the show!'

Janna smiled at Vega with her gappy teeth and patted Flor goodbye. Then she was gone.

'Oh,' said Vega. She'd much rather have gone to watch Phoenix's animal show than stay here with this woman. There was something about the rope charmer that made Vega's stomach turn inside out. And yet she couldn't stop looking at her.

Nelson cleared his throat. 'Well, Ms Ropecharmer, we'd like to ask you a few questions,' he said, looking at the ground.

The rope charmer smiled her secret smile. 'You can call me Ursula.'

'Okay, Mrs Ursula,' said Nelson, 'we'd like to begin by asking how long you've been here at the circus?'

'As long as I can remember,' said Ursula. 'A very long time.'

'I see. Then you might remember something that happened a few years ago.'

'I remember everything as if it was yesterday.'

'Oh, that's nice.'

Nelson fell silent. It was unusual to see him having such difficulty getting his words out. Usually no one could get a word in edgewise once he started, but now he seemed to be struggling. He looked down at the ground and scraped his foot on the grass. Vega cleared her throat. It felt as if there was sawdust in it. Or Hector's dragon candy.

'Do you remember the last circus director?' she asked.

Ursula turned her gaze on her, drilling deep into Vega's forehead.

'What do you want to know?' Ursula asked.

'What happened? Why did he disappear?'

'It was an accident.'

'How did it happen?'

'It's a long story.'

'We've travelled a long way to hear it.'

Ursula came down from her wagon and sat on one of the chairs outside. She moved smoothly, but there was something about her that seemed old, ancient as a mountain. When she began to speak, it was as if the voice came from another place, from deep inside the mountain.

'I've never seen anyone so proud of their job. He was more than a circus director; he was a father. He had such love for everyone at the circus and he made sure they were comfortable and had all they needed. He would never have let anything happen to anyone. But no one can control everything.'

Nelson sat on the ground. Flor lay behind him, her body like a wall around him.

'It was a golden time,' Ursula continued. 'The best in the history of the circus. We travelled the world. The performances were always sold out. What the public didn't know was that it was all due to the circus director. It was thanks to him that our acrobats and jugglers and tightrope walkers were the best in the world. He brought out the best in all of us.'

Ursula paused to look up at the sky. A small snowflake floated down and settled in her open hand. It's too early in the year for snow, thought a voice in Vega's head. It was the grown-up voice that knew how things should be. Dad's voice.

Ursula carried on. 'We were on tour in a warm country

far from here. Velvet-dark evenings. Many people came to watch. It was a normal performance; everything went according to plan. No one could have predicted what happened. The acrobats were in the middle of their act. They did their triple flips high in the air, throwing themselves between the trapezes. The audience held their breath for each jump. The spotlight circled, following the acrobats' dance. But just as one of the acrobats grabbed the trapeze, the rope it was hanging from broke, and she fell. One of the others, heading for the same trapeze, managed to grab a chain hanging from the roof of the tent. The whole tent buckled. The roof came down on the audience and it became pitch black. Everyone started screaming and rushing to get out.'

Several snowflakes now danced lightly from the sky. Flor stuck her tongue out to catch them.

'What happened next?' Vega asked in a low voice.

'There was a commotion. I was standing near an exit, so I was able to get out quickly. Then I saw the circus director in the dark. He ran to his wagon, and a moment later came out with a bundle. Then he disappeared into the dark, and I never saw him again.'

'What was in the bundle?' Vega whispered.

Ursula sighed. She lifted her hand to her black braid, as if it contained the memory, and it hurt.

'It's a terrible story. I don't know why he did it.'

'What do you mean?'

'If he'd only stayed a little longer, he would have understood...'

Ursula looked at the ground for a long time. Then she looked at Vega, and the night sky in her eyes swallowed the whole world around them. 'He had a daughter.'

Vega's heart stopped.

As Ursula went on, her voice seemed to reverberate through an infinite universe. There was no ground to stand on. 'His daughter... She grew up in the circus, she lived and breathed tricks and magic. And she had a very special ability, even as a little girl. An innate talent. The circus director had it too. But he never let her perform. He watched over her as if she were a child, as if he couldn't see that she'd become a full-grown woman. So, she had to content herself with watching the performances. Every night she stood as close to the arena as she could without being in the spotlight. Mostly she wanted to be close to the animals, so she could calm them down before they went on stage. But on this particular evening, she'd climbed one of the scaffolds under the tent roof so she could see the show from above. When the rope broke and the tent collapsed, she fell and ended up under everything.'

Vega, Nelson and Flor all gasped. 'The circus director must have thought she'd died,' Ursula said. 'Maybe he thought everyone'd died, that it was his fault.' Ursula gave a sorry smile.

'But she survived. She hurt herself badly and was

unconscious for a few days. When she woke up, her father, the circus director, was gone. He'd gone without leaving so much as a note. And he'd taken the most important thing she had.'

'What was that?' Vega whispered.

Ursula looked at Vega. The snow now lay in a thin blanket over the ground.

'Her little daughter.'

# 18

# Snails can sleep
# for three years

VEGA'S HEART seemed to stop for several minutes. It went as still as the surface of Giraffe's Heart, when it gleamed without even a ripple.

Nelson was first to find his voice. 'So, the circus director's daughter isn't dead?'

'No,' said Ursula.

'Forgive me for asking, but would it be possible that the daughter...is you?'

Ursula laughed.

'Didn't you hear what I told you? I saw the circus director fleeing with his granddaughter in his arms. His daughter lay injured inside the tent. I was standing outside.'

'Of course, sorry,' said Nelson. 'I get a bit confused if I don't write things down. I've got everything else written in my notebook, I can show...'

Nelson pulled out *Nelson's Mysteries and Such* and began flipping pages and muttering.

A small swirl of snow whirled by. Vega's thoughts went with it. They tore into a fine powder that blended with the snow, did a few laps round Vega, then settled on the ground in front of her. Vega couldn't tell what was snow and what were her thoughts. She bent down and made a snowball. At least now her thoughts had a shape, something she could hold. She remembered how she used to build snow horses and cows at the farm in winter. As soon as she'd formed a ball, they'd build the rest of their bodies themselves and then gallop round the house. But there wasn't the smallest snow calf here. Just a ball full of questions.

'All that remains is the winning question,' said Nelson. He sat cross-legged on the ground with his notebook in his arms. 'Where is the circus director's daughter now?'

'I'd say the winning question is: where is the circus director?' said Ursula.

'I think we can answer that question,' said Nelson. 'Hector is in his Muffinmobile over in the park. We don't really know what he's doing, maybe having a nap. Did you know that snails can sleep for three years in a row? Ants, on the other hand, never sleep, they just work night and day. It's pretty cool actually, once I stayed up for a whole day and night and—'

Ursula stood up so abruptly, her chair fell over. 'Director Hector is back?' she gasped.

'Yes,' said Nelson, a little annoyed at being interrupted. 'But he doesn't seem to want to come here.'

'But we must go to him at once! We've been waiting years for him to come back. I'll gather up the others!'

'Of course.' Nelson made a reassuring gesture. 'We'll take you to him. But first you must tell us where his daughter is.'

Ursula collected herself and took a deep breath.

'She's here. She never left the circus. She has another daughter now. The one who brought you to me.'

Nelson screamed. He sounded like a wounded pig-monkey.

'Janna?!' he cried.

'Yes, Janna. Her mother is Circus Director Hector's daughter.'

Vega dropped her snowball. Big waves were breaking the calm surface of her heart, from a storm far down in the depths, where you can no longer touch the bottom. She felt the storm surge up in her throat, pour on through her mouth and eyes, drowning her face.

Nelson and Flor got up and went to her.

Flor took out a handkerchief. Nelson took Vega's hands in his own. 'I told you it was Katja,' he said quietly. 'As soon as I saw her picture on the programme. I'm as psychic as a koala. Janna was just guessing; she didn't know anything about all this. Katja is clearly your mother. The circus director, just like your grandfather.'

The storm seemed likely to tear Vega apart. She sank to the ground. Her curls fell over her eyes and stuck to her cheeks. So many maybes, so many mothers, all in one day. And now at last she had the answer. From inside the tent the opening music was heard; applause and catcalls died away, replaced by an expectant silence. The show was about to begin.

Then Vega heard it.

All other sounds disappeared.

The wind ceased and the snow stopped falling.

The only sound was a song. A song so beautiful it cut through the storm in Vega's heart and calmed the surface of the water mid-wave. The song found its way into her ears, through her head and out into her curls, into the tips of her fingers, her toes, her knees, her stomach and all the way to the bedroom at home on Giraffe Island, where her father sat in the dark and sang to her softly.

*When the sun's gone down,*
*all I can't see takes a life of its own.*
*Morning always turns to night,*

*whatever begins comes to an end,*
*up goes down and in comes out.*

*I know what it means:*
*Soon the day I'm waiting for will come.*

*When elephants become giraffes*
*and ostriches can fly,*
*when dogs walk on two legs, geese on four,*

*then the day has come, my only friend,*
*the day I'll be with you again.*

Vega got up without a word. She turned towards the circus tent, drawn by the enchantment of the song. Time slowed again, but her steps quickened, and suddenly she was running, faster and faster, ploughing through the heavy air, snow crackling underfoot, the cold deepening every second, but she didn't stop, all she could hear was the song calling her. A horde of animals stood in the door of the tent, blocking her way. Vega squeezed between two zebras, crawled under an elephant's belly, past a hairy llama, and on, between a pair of tigers. A horned bear sat on one of the tigers' backs and waved anxiously at Vega.

Now she could see the light from the arena, she was almost there, so close to seeing who was singing, so close that the song came loud and clear ...

*... then the day has come, my only friend,*
*the day I'll be with you again.*

...when a sound like a thousand shattering glasses cut through her, and a wall of ice appeared, slamming into place in front of her nose. The cold struck like a sledge-hammer. Vega looked up.

Right in her path, white as snow and big as a house, was Viola.

# 19

# Ostriches run faster than horses

SHE WAS TRAPPED. Cold hands gripped like a vice around her arms. The cold went in through her skin to her blood, stiffening her whole body, as if she'd spent hours in a freezer.

She heard her father's voice, ringing like metal: 'Why did you run away, Vega? That was an awful thing to do! We've been so worried!'

Vega didn't dare look up; she could hear that her father wasn't Dad any longer, and she didn't want to see what he'd become.

'Look at me, Vega!' his voice rang out. A frosty hand lifted her chin.

There they were, Dad and Viola, staring at her, their eyes icy. Viola's black hair fell all the way to the ground, and her fingers were long and curved, clamped to her father's hand. And Dad. Vega wanted to close her eyes. He was as white as a ghost, his hair frosty and his big heart a lump of solid ice.

'You'll come home with us right away!' said the metallic voice, and the hands began to drag Vega's rigid body back, away from the tent, away from the song, away from the warmth, just when she was so close, she could almost touch it. Now it was over, and she too would turn to ice, enchanted by Viola in a snowy landscape with no warmth. Vega felt her own heart begin to freeze and solidify like an iced-up puddle.

But just then the grip loosened, and Vega fell to the ground with a thud. She looked up and saw Nelson with a rope that seemed to be moving through the air by itself. It whipped around Viola, coil after coil, wrapping her body.

'Quick, Vega!' called Nelson, panting as he tried to tame the other end of the rope. 'Quicker than an ostrich! Do you know they can run faster than horses?'

Vega scrambled to her feet just as Flor rushed over and hoisted her onto her back. The backpack fell off, but she managed to grab onto Flor's neck fur and hold tight. She looked back to see Viola being coiled tighter and tighter, and her father fighting to loosen the rope. She caught a glimpse of Ursula, who stood half-hidden beside the tent. Ursula nodded at Vega and smiled her secret smile.

Then Flor ran into the tent, and everything went dark.

*... When the sun's gone down*
*all I can't see takes ...*

The singing was growing stronger. The horde of animals made a soft wall in front of Vega and Flor, even denser than before. Flor zigzagged between shaggy legs, squeezed past muzzles and crawled under bellies.

The small pink ponies stood in a cluster and whinnied in excitement as the dog pushed past with Vega on her back. A red-and-yellow rhino snorted and stamped its big foot close to Flor's paw. The animals seemed to never end. The closer they came to the ring, the closer the animals stood, and soon Flor could no longer press forward. They were wedged between a hairy elephant and a bald llama.

The song was only a few metres away from them now, but Vega couldn't see a thing.

*... a life of its own.*
*Morning always turns to night*

The animals began to flow forward in a single throng. There was nothing Vega and Flor could do but flow with them. On, on, with spotlights sweeping the ring ahead, the sawdust smelling of warmth and anticipation.

*whatever begins comes to an end,*
*up goes down and in comes out*

The singing was so close that Vega could almost touch it. The animals walked on. The backs of the elephants swayed, the lions waved their tails, the song echoed around the arena.

> *... I know what it means:*
> *Soon the day I'm waiting for will come.*

They reached the edge of the arena. The animals in front of them divided and went in two directions, circling the spotlight. Flor went straight ahead. The light was blinding. Vega could see nothing at all. She tightened her grip on Flor's ruff and blinked at the bright lights. When she opened her eyes again, she and Flor were in the middle of the arena, with the animals around them in a circle. And only a few metres away stood a woman... someone Vega had never seen. Her back was to them, her hair in a turban. She wore a long green coat. Her arms reached out to the sides, and the animals all seemed to be looking at her and following the pattern she intended. It was the woman who was singing. But who was she? It wasn't Katja; Vega would have recognised her. Then it must be...

'Phoenix!' she gasped aloud. 'It's her!'

The woman fell silent. The public began chattering. From the other side of the ring, Janna stepped into the spotlight. She looked worried.

'What do you mean?' she asked. 'Is Phoenix the one you've been looking for?'

The audience began to buzz like confused bees. Vega didn't know what to say. She couldn't explain anything. She just knew that the song Phoenix sang was the one her father used to sing to her. She'd never heard anyone else sing it.

Phoenix turned around. The spotlight lit her from behind so she looked like an angel, her contours glowing, her face deep in shadow. She was just a silhouette.

The audience held its breath. The animals stood silent and still.

At that moment, Nelson came rushing into the arena. He was puffing, out of breath.

'Vega! I've lost count of all the mothers now, but just pick one, and hurry! Right now, Viola is trapped, but not for long! We need the cure for Code V now! $X + Z$ = four thousand billion! It's urgent!'

Nelson ran up to Phoenix and grabbed her hand. 'Hello, I'm Nelson nice to meet you how long have you been at the Circus do you have a birthmark please come with me here it's very important I'll explain everything later!' he babbled as he dragged her out of the spotlight.

The animals stepped aside to let them go. Vega, Flor and Janna followed. As they made their way to the tent opening, the bewildered audience burst into applause.

# Jellyfish are immortal

VEGA SAT RIGID on Flor's back. Nelson went in front, holding Phoenix by the hand. Vega still hadn't seen her face. It was as if Nelson were walking beside a living paper doll. He turned around and hissed: 'What do you think? Is it her?'

Vega nodded.

Nelson made a victory sign with his free hand and laughed:

'We did it, Vega! The whole mystery, we solved it! We found her! Now we just need to get her to warm up your dad, and everything will be back to normal!'

Vega had an uneasy feeling in her stomach. She was no longer sure that this was the right solution. Janna came running after them and was about to say something, but she stopped at the sight of what awaited them outside the tent.

Viola was still bound by the rope. An angry snowstorm

swirled around her, and Vega's father, vainly trying to loosen the rope, stood in a snowdrift that reached his waist.

Phoenix let go of Nelson's hand and put her hands to her face when she saw Viola and Dad.

'Aaron!' she gasped, as if she'd seen a ghost. Dad froze and turned his head. Vega could see his heart trembling through his jacket, as if something wanted to burst through the ice. Was it Phoenix's warmth that did it? The cloud above Dad's head was part of a blizzard now.

But somewhere it must have been raining because Vega saw water rising in his eyes.

'What are you doing here?' Phoenix's voice trembled.

'I'm trying to look after my daughter,' said Dad.

'Your daughter?'

'Yes, my daughter. Vega. If you remember.' Dad nodded in Vega's direction.

'Vega?' whispered Phoenix. 'No, Vega . . . she disappeared, I searched . . .'

Phoenix looked around in confusion. Vega was still sitting on Flor's back, a few steps behind Phoenix. She almost hardly dared watch the paper doll turn around. This was the moment it would have a face, a real face that would never be blurry again, no clown nose that could fall off, no wings of fire or shoes that were too big. She closed her eyes and buried her face in Flor's fur, clinging to the dog with her legs and arms.

'Vega, is that really you?'

The voice was right next to Vega's face. She squinted cautiously through Flor's neck fur. She was met by the very eyes that had looked at her so many times from the portrait on Hector's stove. Big, dark, and so full of all the world's questions and worries that Vega almost couldn't face them. But there were faint sun-ray lines at the corners of her eyes. Phoenix had large earrings with tiny bells in them that tinkled, and a few short dark curls stuck out from her turban.

Phoenix reached out and gently stroked Vega's hair. 'Vega, I can't believe it. My daughter. You're here.'

They were interrupted by a loud shriek. It was Viola. The rope had tightened around her even more. Vega looked around for Ursula. The snake charmer's eyes blinked at her from behind a tree. Vega didn't know if she should blink back.

'But who is this poor woman, all tied up?' cried Phoenix.

Vega straightened on Flor's back.

'It's not a woman!' she cried. 'It's an ice queen!'

'Yep, an ice queen!' Nelson agreed. 'She's evil and dangerous!'

'We came to get you,' Vega told Phoenix, 'so you can come home with us and be with Dad again so he'll be freed from the ice queen's spell!'

It sounded different when she said it aloud. The words just flopped out and lay flat on the ground. The only one who reacted as they should was Nelson, who did a triumphant pirouette, landing on one knee, with both arms outstretched.

'Ta-daaaaa!' he said.

Vega's father took a deep breath in, then breathed out the biggest sigh she had ever heard.

'No,' he said. 'She's no ice queen. This is Viola, my girlfriend. Vega, I've been trying to tell you, she is no danger to you.'

'She is a danger!' cried Vega to Phoenix. 'The ice queen is moving into our apartment, and everything is cold and terrible! Dad has changed completely! You have to come back to us so you can warm him up again! You're the only answer!'

The words sounded even flatter this time. She looked at Nelson, who was still in his triumphant pose on the ground. He nodded encouragingly.

'Yep, the only logically possible solution,' he added. 'After many extensive calculations and investigations. You can see my diagram.'

Phoenix looked as if she was swallowing every word. She walked silently up to Viola.

'Let go!' Phoenix said decisively and the rope fell to the ground, lifeless. Vega looked around for Ursula. She was gone.

Viola whimpered and Dad hugged her. The rope had scraped some of the ice from her body. It was dripping. 'I'm sorry you got dragged into this,' said Dad, turning to

Phoenix. 'I had no idea she'd come looking for you. She ran away from home. We had to contact her school, where we learned she had a pen pal who lives at a circus.'

Phoenix looked at Janna, who'd stood silently throughout this conversation. Vega had almost forgotten she was there. Janna raised her hand and gave a shy little smile.

'I knew nothing about it,' Dad went on. 'Vega has been acting so strangely ever since I started seeing Viola. But perhaps it's not surprising that she has trouble trusting someone who only wants to be her mother, considering that her real mother abandoned her.'

Dad's voice was sharp. Hard, jagged icicles.

'Abandoned?' Phoenix gasped. 'What makes you think I abandoned her?

'One fine day nine years ago, there was a knock on my door. It was some people in white coats, with a baby in their arms.'

People in white. The agents.

'They said it was my daughter, put the baby in my arms and left. Your father was standing behind them.'

'Hector?' Phoenix whispered, and she sounded small, like the little girl in the picture.

'Yes,' said Dad. 'He told me the child was called Vega and that he couldn't take care of her. And that you couldn't either. That you were gone.'

'Speaking of children,' Nelson interjected, 'did you know that some jellyfish can evolve from the adult stage back to the juvenile stage? So, they're basically immortal! That's good, huh?'

No one took any notice.

'He was the one who'd gone,' said Phoenix, shaking her head. 'And Vega. They disappeared. I did all I could to find them, but it was hopeless. The police couldn't do anything, we were in a foreign country, I had no idea where they were. I put up notices everywhere we went, but it was as if they'd gone up in smoke. All I could do was hope that Hector would come back with Vega one day. But he must have lost his mind. I don't know why he took her with him.'

Vega couldn't stand it any longer.

'Can you stop talking about me as if I'm not here!' she cried, hopping off Flor's back. 'I've never been away; I've been right here all the time! You're the ones who've been gone! And Hector hasn't lost his mind! He's the only one who's ever understood me!'

She stepped forward and put her foot on something hard. She looked down to see her sketchpad. Beside it was the backpack she'd dropped when she jumped onto Flor's back. The sketchpad was open to a page with a big green giraffe with elephant ears.

Phoenix crouched beside her.

'What's this? Are these your drawings?' she asked softly.
Vega nodded.

'They're lovely. Absolutely beautiful. *When elephants become giraffes...*' Phoenix sang the line, while her fingers traced the drawing of the green giraffe. '*Then the day has come, my only friend, the day I am with you again.*'

Dad came over and squatted beside them. Small shards of ice fell from his bent legs.

'I didn't know you drew, Vega,' he said cautiously.

'You never want to know anything about my animals,' said Vega, still looking down. 'You just want me to go outside and skip.'

Phoenix and Dad were silent for a moment.

'It's interesting, Vega,' Phoenix then said. 'I know these animals. I've met them too. You seem to have inherited my imagination.'

Vega didn't want to look up. Drops were falling on the drawings. The green giraffe was blurry when she looked at it.

'It's lovely, isn't it?' Phoenix continued. 'There's so much to see. And we never have to feel lonely or bored. But sometimes they can be a bit... in the way. It's not always convenient to be visited by so many fantastic creatures, especially when others can't see what we see. Do you recognise that feeling?'

Vega nodded.

Phoenix touched Vega's cheek.

'I want to show you something,' she whispered.

# The giraffe's heart is unusually large

PHOENIX HELD OUT her hand. Vega hesitated, and her eyes fell on Janna. She wondered what Janna thought about everything. Maybe she'd dismissed the idea of Katja being Vega's mother, because she simply didn't want Vega and Nelson to take away either of her mothers? Janna smiled at Vega and nodded. A warm breeze caressed Vega's cheek. Flor came and stood close, so Vega could feel her warm fur against her body. The dog nuzzled Vega's arm a little. Vega gave Phoenix her hand.

Time stopped, just like in the apartment when Vega had run away from home. But it felt different. It wasn't scary. It just was. Dad stood frozen, his hands mid-gesture. Viola was frozen in time as if the rope still bound her. Janna stood motionless. Even Nelson was still, in his triumphant position on the ground, on one knee with his hands outstretched. Flor too had stiffened, her big soft head next to Vega's body. Vega patted her fur, and then turned to Phoenix. Phoenix squeezed Vega's hand, and they began to walk.

Phoenix took Vega to a small empty patch of grass some distance away. Everything was quiet and still around them.

'What do you see?' Phoenix asked.

Vega looked at the empty field. There was just one little grassling, asleep. Or maybe it was petrified like the others.

'Nothing,' she replied.

'Are you sure?'

Vega knew the lawn was empty. There were no grasslings, no chickadoodles, asphalt beavers, spoonlurks or moaners. She'd understood that. They weren't in any encyclopaedia, and they made Dad's rooftop eyebrows rain. There were no mammoths in the wardrobe, no polar bears in her bedroom. Dad had said so. Many times.

'Yes, I'm sure,' she said. 'Just grass.'

Phoenix giggled. 'I see a very cute little grassling lying asleep,' she said. 'Can't you see it?'

Vega was speechless. She looked wide-eyed at Phoenix. Phoenix's eyes sparkled, and a big smile lit up her whole face. The paper doll was no longer a paper doll. Here she was, alive. Or maybe she was also like the grassling, not quite real?

'Look again,' said Phoenix. 'Sometimes you have to be very still and look very carefully to see things.'

Vega looked at the grassling again. It wasn't petrified. She could hear muffled snoring and see its stomach moving calmly with each breath.

Suddenly, it woke with a yawn, stretched and began to grunt and snuffle around the small patch of grass. From a bush, a fourfentipede waddled out and bumped into the grassling. The fourfentipede looked offended and started to roar, but soon calmed down. They sniffed each other, then each went their way. From a thicket came frustrated snorts, and Vega saw a small herd of pygmy hippos coming at a gallop. They moved elegantly, despite their short legs. From the same direction, two musclehorns were striding, hand in hand. Vega had only ever seen them beside the small pond in Hector's garden, where they were always trying to empty the pond by filling their mouths with water and squirting it onto the lawn. Behind the musclehorns were bats, a chicka-doodle, a whole bunch of little string puppies, and some fuzzy soapvandals buzzing and tripping over each other. The grass was full of animals!

'You see them, don't you, Vega?' Phoenix asked, crouching on the grass.

'Yes,' breathed Vega, 'I see them. I've drawn them all in my sketchbook. The grassling, the fourfentipede, the chickadoodle . . . But I've never seen so many dwarf wobblers at the same time!'

She couldn't help giggling.

'I know,' said Phoenix, with a bubbly laugh, like sweet mulled wine coming to the boil. Vega felt sure that Nelson would want to record that laugh. 'Do you mean the ones that look almost like short-legged camels? Dwarf wobblers, what a good name. I've never known what they were called. But I see them everywhere in this park.'

'So, you mean you can see all these animals too?' asked Vega.

'Sure,' said Phoenix. 'You seem to have inherited it from me. As I inherited it from my father, your grandfather.'

Hector. For the hundredth time today the thought of him stung Vega.

'And do you know,' Phoenix went on, 'I learned a trick a long time ago.' She leaned close to Vega's ear and lowered her voice, even though there was no one else to hear. She smelt warm, like earth.

'I discovered that if I sing to the animals that I see, others can see them too.'

Vega couldn't believe her ears. Phoenix giggled.

'Haven't you noticed that the animals at this circus are pretty unusual?'

Vega thought about the pink ponies, the checked rhinoceroses and the sabre-toothed tigers. But they were similar to the animals she saw at home on Giraffe Island. She said nothing.

'Didn't you notice that there were mammoths and crossing-zebras in the arena?' said Phoenix. 'Green stone lions and pink ponies, that all the animals were a little . . . special?'

Vega still said nothing. She hadn't given a thought to whether the animals she'd met in the ring were more or less unusual; she'd been focused only on seeing Phoenix.

A baby soapvandal jumped into Vega's arms and went straight to sleep.

'All the animals you saw, the audience could also see, although it's hard to believe. I only choose animals that people can recognise in some way. A checked rhinoceros doesn't cause as much of a stir as a soapvandal, oddly enough.'

Phoenix scratched the little soapvandal between the ears. 'The song I sang in the arena just now brings the whole herd of animals together,' she continued. 'It makes the audience happy, and the animals too.

'But wait,' said Vega. 'How do you fit all the animals in your wagons when you travel to the next place?'

Phoenix laughed and touched Vega's cheek. The sun rays smiled at her.

'They're only visible for as long as I want them to be.'

'What happens to them when they disappear?'

'Puff! They go up in smoke. Or fog, rather. Some I can still see. They wander off, into the park and on with their lives. Or wherever it is they go when even you and I can't see them.'

Puff. Vega had earlier wondered if her mother's warmth

and father's water would just turn into smoke. But it wasn't the kind of smoke she'd imagined.

'I'll show you how to do it!' said Phoenix, hugging Vega's shoulders. 'I remember singing the song to your dad when we met. I told him what it did to the animals, but he didn't seem to believe me. He's a fine man, your father, and he has a big heart, but he doesn't have the same gift as you and me.'

Vega smiled as she thought about Dad, and how afraid he was of all of Vega's animals. The circle of chalk around the dining table. The rooftop eyebrows and the rain clouds. And yet, he'd remembered Phoenix's song, and had sung it to Vega every night.

'I knew even before I realised I was having you that he and I couldn't live together. But when we parted, I understood that I'd received a wonderful gift from him. You.'

It was raining again, and Phoenix was blurry when Vega looked at her. Vega wiped the rain from her eyes with the back of her hand.

'And you have my imagination; I noticed it in you when you were a little baby. You used to lie in your bed and laugh at the flying hamsters buzzing on the ceiling. I knew you saw the same things I did.'

Vega didn't know what to say. It made her ache to hear Phoenix's story. To think that she'd been a little baby laughing at flying hamsters in one of the circus wagons. She wished she could remember it. All she remembered was Giraffe Island, and Dad, and a whole life where no one understood what she saw. Except Hector.

'I've thought about you so much, Vega. You've been like a little paper doll in my head, I've tried to imagine what you would look like and how you'd be. Now I finally get to see you, and you're more beautiful than anything I could have imagined!'

The paper doll in Vega's head had Phoenix's face now, Phoenix's smell, Phoenix's laugh, and her wonderful singing voice. It stretched and the paper turned into skin: warm, real skin. Vega reached out her hand and touched the woman crouching beside her. Her mother. The arm was soft and real. And there, under one sleeve of the green coat, was a giraffe-shaped birthmark. It was slightly larger than the one on Vega's arm. The giraffe winked at Vega, as if to say, 'Good job, you found me.'

Phoenix and Vega started walking slowly back to the others. Vega had no idea how long they'd been gone, but Dad, Viola, Nelson, Janna and Flor were still in the same moment they'd left them.

'I know I've missed a lot, Vega,' said Phoenix. 'Well, I've missed everything. I wish I could have been there and taken care of you. If only I'd known where you were.'

Phoenix squeezed Vega's hand in hers. Vega heard her take a deep breath. It sounded like there was rain in her lungs now too.

'But it seems you've had a very good time anyway. What

a wonderful dad you have who worries about you and looks for you when you run away. I promise that from now on, you'll have me too.'

They reached the others, who were slowly coming back to life. Vega blinked a little to shake off the last raindrops. She looked into Phoenix's eyes, which were like the saddest, darkest forest stars you could imagine. Then she looked at Dad. The ice in his eyes had begun to melt and was running in wild spring streams down his cheeks. The skin on his face had regained its colour and steamed a little where the spring streams had thawed the ice. They ran all the way down to his heart, where the ice had finally given way and the waves had pushed through.

Her father's heart was big and blue again; it pounded and surged far beyond his jacket. It was like a sea where all the world's sorrows could be drowned. Or they could grow gills and take on a new life as something else. Dad's throat suddenly grew a few metres and his skin became mottled, and he looked suddenly very much like a giraffe. Because a giraffe's heart is unusually large, Hector had said. And Dad really did have a heart as big as a giraffe's.

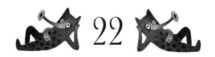

# 22

# There are
# a hundred million
# animal species

IT WAS SNOWING AGAIN. But it was a different kind of snow now. It didn't feel cold. Across the park, Vega saw a whole family of polar bears lumbering along, and behind the circus tent a huge hairy mammoth roared and tossed a snowdrift about with its trunk. Vega glanced at Phoenix, who winked back.

Nelson was inspecting Viola with his magnifying glass.

'You know, Vega,' said Nelson. 'I'm not entirely sure she's colder than anyone else. I was more or less expecting a solid block of ice.'

Nelson poked Viola's arm with a finger. Viola looked a little uneasy at first, but then she smiled. A small, friendly smile that softened her face.

'Or maybe the formula took everything cold into account,' Nelson continued to speculate. 'Maybe $x + 24v - 0° + y = 100\%$ should really be $x + 24v - 0° + y =$ a thousand billion percent, so that adding factor x melted the original cause of the ice as well. It's hard to know. Or maybe it's just that summer's coming.'

Viola somehow didn't look cold anymore. She'd shrunk, her hands no longer looked like claws, and her cheeks had little rosebuds in them. They looked as if they could bloom at any moment. Dad wrapped his arms around her. 'Are you okay?' he asked, and Viola nodded, looking at him.

And now there was no longer a blizzard joining them together, no ice over Dad's eyes. Instead, Vega saw little pink hearts sail down from Dad's cloud and spin a few circuits around Viola. They looked as if they were made of thin tissue paper. They floated down and melted into little pink spots in the snow.

'I think we should go and find Hector,' said Vega.

'Hector?' Phoenix gasped. 'Is he still alive?'

'He's the most living grandfather this side of the Kola Peninsula!' Nelson grinned. 'We drove here in his Muffinmobile!'

'Come on, we'll go and find him.' Vega took Phoenix by the hand. They began walking towards the field.

'Wait for me!'

Janna came running after them and Vega held out her other hand to her.

'Janna, I think we're more than pen pals,' she said. 'I think we may be sisters.'

'I've always wanted a sister!' said Janna. 'And suddenly you have more mothers than you can count!'

Phoenix laughed loudly.

'Right, let's see what Katja has to say about all this!'

'Yeehah!' Nelson cried as he rode by on Flor's back.

Behind them came Dad and Viola. A little behind them were a couple of zebras. Next was a bunch of clowns, then some tightrope walkers, a magician and four acrobats doing somersaults. Vega saw Olga the fire-eater and Cindy the clown in the crowd. The rumour that the old circus director was back had spread through the circus like the sun's warmth. More and more artists came out of the tent and started to follow Vega and the others across the field.

The Muffinmobile was right where they'd left it.

Hector was nowhere to be seen.

'Hector!' Vega shouted.

They saw tracks in the snow, going from the Muffinmobile towards a grove of trees. One of the bottles that Flor had filled with water from Giraffe's Heart had been tossed on the ground. Vega picked it up. Empty.

They followed the tracks until they abruptly ended at a tree. Vega looked up.

'Hector?'

'Ahoy!' Hector's voice came from high in the treetops. 'Have you finished your little excursion now?'

'Yes,' Vega said with a laugh. 'Finished. Come on down, we have someone who wants to meet you.'

'Have you found any exciting animals here in the park? I imagine so, Vega, small figment of my imagination, since you have the eyes of an albatross!'

A pair of feet came stepping down the trunk.

'Well, I've been picking a few keys to freeze for winter,' Hector carried on talking as he came down. 'They're a bit wilted, but if we soak them, they'll be fine . . .'

Hector moved as if climbing trees was all he'd ever done. A metre from the ground, he leaped from the trunk and landed on all fours, like a panther. Some frudbimbles flapped from the tree and settled at his feet. Hector stood up and proudly held out a bunch of keys. In the same moment, he saw Phoenix.

'Oh! It can't be . . . !'

The keys fell to the ground with a thud.

'Yes, Dad,' said Phoenix. 'It really is me, Phoenix.'

'Oh, Phoenix! I thought you were . . . I mean, I had no idea . . .'

Hector looked as if he'd seen a ghost. His mouth kept opening but no sound came out.

'I know,' said Phoenix, 'gently does it, Dad.'

'You disappeared; I thought you . . . you'd . . . I thought you'd died.'

'No, I'm alive, as you can see. You were the one who disappeared.'

'I thought... I don't really remember what happened ...
Is it really you?'

'Don't you know me? Look here then!'

Phoenix rolled up one sleeve of her coat and held out her
bare arm. The upside-down giraffe looked shyly at Hector.
Nelson rushed up with his magnifying glass.

'The birthmark! The core of the whole mystery! I knew
I'd figure it out!'

Hector's face was breaking into an enormous smile.
He went to Phoenix and cradled her face in his hands.
'It is you! My own girl. How big you've grown! You used
to be so small.'

'That was long ago, Dad. Vega's the small one now.'

'Small? Yes, she was tiny, a little baby who would have
grown up without a mother. I couldn't leave her there,
oh... it was all my fault...'

Phoenix closed her eyes, then shook her head and
breathed out a little laugh before cutting him off.

'I'm just glad you found your way here at last.'

Suddenly a trunk tapped Hector on the shoulder.
He turned to see a huge elephant with a tousled topknot.
'Mabel!' he exclaimed. 'It's you! What a long time it's been!'

'It has, and there are many others wanting to see you,'
said Phoenix.

All the other animals and circus performers who'd
hung back, watching, came to Hector now. The people
laughed and cried as they hugged him. Then they lifted

him into the air and carried him over the field towards the circus tent.

VEGA WAS LEFT standing under the key tree. Dad came up to her with his lanky giraffe neck. He crouched and gently put an arm around her.

'How are you doing, Vega?'

'I really don't get it,' she said.

'What don't you get?'

'Everything. Where did the ice go? What happened to your cloud? How could Hector have forgotten the circus? Why were you so angry with my mother when she was just sad? I don't get how it all fits together.'

'I'm not sure I do either,' said Dad, scratching his head. 'Maybe there's no easy answer.'

'But why did Viola look like an ice queen? And you were completely frozen. I got so scared. It felt like everything was breaking up, and I was the only one who could fix it. But it doesn't feel that way anymore. Everything's still messy, though.'

Dad hugged Vega.

'It is messy,' he said, stroking her hair. 'And that's how it is. It's not always easy to understand what you feel. It's the heart's fault.'

'Especially if your heart is in your head, like Nelson says mine is,' said Vega into her father's shoulder.

'Yes, that makes it especially hard,' said Dad, laughing. 'You can't always resist your heart. It can storm and rage at times, blowing from all directions at once, so it's hard to see where you're going. It's the heart that decides, and yet the heart doesn't always know best. It can be unreliable, stubborn, and sometimes impossible to deal with.'

Vega thought of the elephant walking around the china shop. 'The heart is tricky,' Dad continued thoughtfully. 'It can fool you. You think you know where you are for a moment, but then suddenly a sea monster swims up out of the dark, and messes you about, just when you thought you were swimming in the right direction.'

Dad put a hand to Vega's chest. Inside her jacket she still had the photograph of her and Dad that she'd taken from the fridge.

'The heart can hurt,' Dad said quietly. 'So badly you think it's broken. Like a huge iceberg crumpling into the sea. Or like hard rain, with drops striking the surface like arrows and drilling down deep until the pain becomes part of the heart, the way rain becomes part of the sea.'

Vega looked up and saw that it was raining over Dad's rooftop eyebrows. She reached up and wiped away the wet.

'The heart can freeze, like after a long winter,' he went on, 'and you can't imagine it will ever warm again. You just have to wait for the sun, and hope it melts the ice.'

Dad took in a big, sighing breath.

'But nothing lasts forever. If a winter can turn into

summer, a broken heart can mend. And even though you sometimes wish your heart would behave a little more like other people's, it's quite exciting to see where it takes you. Every day it comes up with something new. It's mysterious, and vast. Infinite, actually. Bottomless and endless.'

'Just like Giraffe's Heart,' said Vega, wrapping her arms around Dad's neck. She could feel his heart pounding, through his jacket and right up into the trees, which shuddered as if in an earthquake.

Nelson and Flor came up to them. 'Well, what happens now?' Nelson asked.

'I'm hungry,' said Vega.

'Me too,' said Nelson. 'I haven't eaten anything since the Muffinmobile muffins this morning. If I were a tapeworm, I'd have eaten myself a long time ago.'

'I'm sure you can conjure up some food, you master detective,' laughed Vega. She put her arm around Nelson in his blue overalls.

'You did it!' she said. 'You solved the Circature Mystery!'

'Nah. I don't know about that. I should probably stick to my fact book. *Nelson's Mysteries and Such* never had the same punch as *Nelson's Interesting Facts*. I'm also quite keen on writing a book about circus performers' various birthmarks. There might be several here who have cool ones.'

'I thought *Nelson's Mysteries and Such* was great. Maybe one day you can write a whole book about this mystery, and include a lot of fun facts?'

'Good idea! Huh, but how will I choose? There are so many strange and funny facts about animals. Did you know, for example, that there are at least a hundred million animal species?'

'True?'

'Maybe.'

Vega looked at the sketchbook sticking out from her jacket pocket.

'If you write about our adventure, may I draw the pictures?'

# Epilogue

DID YOU KNOW that giraffes can't swim? Probably everyone knows that by now. They don't usually live near water, so they've had no reason to learn. They're quite happy roaming around the savannah with their high blood pressure, blue tongue and long neck, nibbling fresh shoots from the treetops. Why would a giraffe need to be able to swim?

Far out to sea, which may well be the very sea you're imagining, is an island, which may well be the very one you're thinking of. If you look at the island from above, say from the back of an albatross, you can see that it's shaped like a giraffe. It has three legs and a small tail, a large body, and a long neck with a head. Around the body, the sea is as blue as a giraffe's tongue, and moose swim alongside seahorses and passenger ferries on their way to or from the island. In the middle of the body is a large lake, called Giraffe's Heart.

The lake is unusually large for such a small island, just as the giraffe's heart is unusually large for its body. If you fly your albatross a little closer to Giraffe's Heart, you can see that the surface is shiny and still, and that a mist is slowly spreading over the water. Or is it smoke? People have gathered at the beach, small as ants, going back and forth with their little ant boxes, building little ant houses that look like sweets along the shore. Of course, they're not little sweets but real houses, and the ants are normal-sized people. But where has the fog come from? Fly closer. You'll see some children playing in the fog. Of course, it's hard to hear what's being said on the ground when you're up on an albatross. But you can probably guess that it's something like this:

POOF!

'Oh, couldn't it stay just a bit longer? It was so cute!' says a tall boy in blue overalls, bouncing in excitement. 'We can call him Nelson.'

'Yes, sing it again, Vega, please!' A girl with wavy blonde hair laughs in a way that makes her teeth whistle. Her name is Janna.

Janna runs up to the third child, the one standing and singing. It's a girl with dark, curly hair and a slightly worried look. She has a birthmark on one arm in the shape of a giraffe.

It's Vega.

'I haven't learned how to make them stay very long,' says Vega, clearing her throat.

'Can't you bring back the little one with spikes on its head and wings?' Janna asks.

'You mean the horned bear?'

'Yes!'

PUFF!

'And then that one with the long trunk and a tuft of grass on its head!' Nelson says, practically dancing.

'The tufted snozzrambler? I'll try!'

POOF!

The mist made by all the animals going up in smoke settles thickly over the lake, like candyfloss.

'Don't stop, Vega!'

POOF!

An old man with a lot of curly hair comes walking along with a small trolley. The trolley hums like a cake-mixer. A round hat sits on a shelf on the trolley.

'Hector, can the trolley make more muffins?' asks Nelson.

'Do you want me to run around non-stop?' asks Hector. 'It's one muffin per hundred steps with this thing, you know, it's not the Muffinmobile. But sure, it's undeniably a motivating pedometer.'

The trolley makes a hiss, and out comes a small plate with one perfect, piping-hot blueberry muffin.

'Hands off, bluenose!' Hector says. 'This one's for Vega. Take a bite, small figment of my imagination, and then you can sing up that sorrowful grey mara awaiting her turn, over by the cliff.'

Vega takes a bite of the muffin and sings a few notes through crumbs.

'She's cute!' says Nelson. 'I thought she'd be scary!'

The grey mara that appears is so surprised by the compliment she forgets to look miserable, and her little mouth turns up into a shy smile. Hector drops to his knees and makes his fizzing laugh.

'Number thirty-four,' Nelson says quickly into his tape recorder before holding it at Hector.

'Perfect! Like a bun that's dry, but good,' he says when Hector has finished laughing.

'I know,' says Janna, 'why don't we go around singing up funny animals, so you can record everyone's laughs?'

They all run from the shore up to the construction site. A skeleton of planks and boards forms the silhouette of a house, and at the top of a plank, beside what looks to be a roof, a woman in yellow overalls is hammering. Her red hair is tied in a big ponytail, and she's muttering quietly to herself as she aims at a nail.

'Katja, how's it going?' Janna calls from below.

'Oh, making progress!' Katja shouts from the scaffolding. 'But tell Phoenix to sing me up an elephant soon so I can come down! Isn't it lunchtime yet?'

'There are muffins if you're hungry!' Nelson shouts, then whispers to Vega, 'Now sing up something really silly!'

Vega sings a few notes, and a small round creature with a trumpet mouth appears on the plank where Katja is sitting. It honks triumphantly right in her face, then goes up in smoke with a POOF.

Katja claps her hands and laughs in a roar that ruffles the glassy surface of Giraffe's Heart. Nelson holds up his tape recorder.

'Number thirty-five!' he says joyfully. 'Like thunder!'

'When I come down, you'll have me to deal with,' Katja calls out between gasps of laughter. 'See if you can scare Phoenix too!'

The children giggle and go on across the planks of the skeleton house, over stones and puddles until they reach a patch of grass with a caravan. The door is open, and outside sits a woman in a turban with a huge golden-haired dog. The dog is rinsing potatoes, picking them up carefully one at a time and passing them to the woman, who peels them. The woman chats to the dog, pausing between sentences as if the dog is answering. When she sees the children, the dog takes a cheese sandwich from a plate and runs to meet the boy, Nelson.

'Oh, thanks Flor, I'm really hungry!' Nelson takes the sandwich from the dog's mouth. 'Hey Phoenix!'

'Hi,' says Phoenix. 'What are you all up to? Lunch won't be long. We just need to build a fire and boil the potatoes.'

'How will you start a fire?' Nelson asks between mouthfuls.

'I'll have to sing up a dragon,' says Phoenix with a wink.

'It won't work on her,' Nelson whispers to Vega. 'We'll have to try something else.'

'Phoenix,' Vega asks, 'what's the strangest animal you know?'

'That's a good question,' says Phoenix, smiling. 'You know yourself how very many there are.'

'But might there be some you haven't seen?' asks Janna, scratching Flor between the ears. 'Like one that only lives here on Giraffe Island? You haven't lived here very long.'

'Quite possible. Who knows what's hiding in these woods.' Phoenix went on peeling potatoes. 'Do you want to help gather wood for the fire?'

Vega's expression suddenly changes, her eyes widen, and she gasps for breath. Her gaze is fixed on something behind the caravan, between the trees. As if she's seen something.

'What is it?' Janna whispers to her.

'I don't know if she'll laugh, but she'll be surprised for sure,' Vega whispers back.

'What, what have you seen?' Nelson hisses. 'Sing, so we can see it too!'

Vega sings a few tentative notes, and from out of the woods, behind the caravan, tumbles a giant creature. It walks on two legs and has long matted hair covering its eyes and a snout that sniffs intently. Its arms are so long that its hands almost touch the ground, and at the end of its hairy legs are two enormous paws the size of sailing dinghies.

'Wha...what on earth?' Nelson stops chewing.

'That, wow, that is actually a humplefoot,' says Vega. 'I never thought I'd ever see one.'

The gigantic fuzzball lumbers towards the back of the caravan, swivelling about as if it's had too many sugary drinks. Phoenix, who sits calmly peeling potatoes with her back to the caravan, is the only one who hasn't seen it. The children hold their breath. It's like watching a speeding train that has derailed and is about to collide with . . . well, a caravan. And then, just as the humplefoot reaches the caravan, it trips over its own feet, pitches over the roof, and falls off the caravan, snout-down in the bowl of potatoes!

Phoenix screams and leaps up. For a moment she's petrified, drenched in potato water. Then laughter bubbles up in her, like a pot coming to the boil, and she laughs and laughs until tears run down her cheeks. Nelson runs up excitedly with the tape recorder.

'Number thirty-six!'

Flor creeps over to the humplefoot, who lies moaning on the ground. She sniffs it gingerly, then backs away and sneezes so hard that her nose hits the ground.

'Oh Flor, you're allergic to humplefeet!' Vega says.

'That counts as a laugh!' Nelson exclaims, taking the tape recorder to the dog. Flor sneezes again. 'Number thirty-seven!'

'Soon you'll be up to forty,' says Janna.

'Yes, and when Vega's dad and Viola come, we'll catch their laughs too.'

POOF!

The humplefoot goes up in smoke. But Vega can still see the creature as it recovers. Embarrassed and confused, it makes its way quickly down to Giraffe's Heart beach. It stumbles and trips repeatedly over its huge feet, howling with a sound that is heart-breaking.

Phoenix comes up beside Vega and watches the creature. 'What kind of animal is that?' she asks.

'That's the humplefoot,' says Vega. 'Hector always told me about it, but I'd never seen it.'

'The humplefoot! He told me about it too when I was little. He said it only existed in one place in the whole world, near a special sweet-water lake.'

The humplefoot has almost reached the shore by the

time Hector sees it. He gets up from his little trolley where he's been sitting eating the remains of Vega's muffin.

'By all the long-tailed spoonlurks!' he exclaims.

The humplefoot stops howling and turns. It looks puzzled to see the old man.

'How rude of me.' Hector fumbles for the hat on his trolley. He places it on his curly hair, then nods and bows at the same time.

'It's an honour to meet you,' he says.

The humplefoot laughs with a hoarse snort and seems surprised by the noise. It laughs again. And again, louder, and louder. The rumbling, raspy sound rolls out over the lake in an echo that makes the surface of the water rise and roil. And from the forest around Giraffe's Heart, hordes of animals suddenly appear. Big, small, green, red, four-legged, two-legged, six-legged, fairy-legged.

Roaring, howling, yelping, honking. They converge on the beach from all directions, jumping, bouncing, splashing, and diving into the water.

'The others have to see this,' says Vega, taking Phoenix by the hand.

They sing together as they walk towards the lake.

'Wild walruses!' Nelson shouts. He runs as fast as he can to the humplefoot, who is bent over, laughing his head off. Nelson raises his tape recorder.

'Number thirty-eight,' he says, trying not to laugh

himself. 'This will definitely be a favourite in the collection! Earthquake with fireworks!'

Vega and Phoenix reach Hector. The sound of the swimming animals forms a carpet of chatter, a kind of rough thrumming that's almost a song.

'It's amazing how many animals live on this island,' says Phoenix. 'Look, there are rock puppies and sea pigs swimming alongside dolphins and seahorses, all in the same water.'

'Yes, they thrive here,' says Hector. 'I always say that this is where all love comes from.'

'And the sugar drink,' says Vega. They look out over Giraffe's Heart.

'I love seeing them all together,' Vega says. 'Spoonlurks, pallervants, bear seals, humblerags, giraffes and...'

Giraffes!

They can't swim, can they?

But sure enough, there's the giraffe, its long lanky neck swaying above the water. As if it's never done anything else. We'll take this as a sign that we've seen enough now. When giraffes start swimming in their own hearts, it's probably time to leave.

GUIDE YOUR ALBATROSS into the sky again. Go way up high, until the wind drowns out the song and chatter from Giraffe's Heart.

From here, it just looks like a lake again. An unusually large lake, in the middle of a small island.

Fly high enough that you can see Capital City, Narrowneck and the Torso forming the three-legged giraffe. Red rocks, like markings on the giraffe's neck. And the big heart at the centre of the body.

The sea spangles in the sun as if a wealthy lady has spilled all her pearls and jewels across the water, and the clouds are as light as cotton balls. It's a beautiful day.

Where shall we fly to now?